THE FANCHOR STORY

THE FANCHOR STORY

How Fananchors fanned Sarkari narrative fantastically

MUKESH BHARDWAJ

YATRA BOOKS
An imprint of Vani Prakashan Group

vaniprakashan.com

Hardbound First Edition , 2024

Yatra Books is an imprint of Vani Prakashan Group

Head Office

4695, 21-A, Daryaganj, New Delhi-110 002, India
Phone : +91 11 23273167, 11 23275710

Registered Bookstores and Offices

Ashok Rajpath, Patna-800 004, Bihar
Coffee House Campus, Mahatma Gandhi Marg, Prayagraj-211 001, Uttar Pradesh
Mahatma Gandhi Antarrashtriya Hindi VishwaVidyalaya, Wardha-442 001, Maharashtra

sales@vaniprakashan.in
vaniprakashan@gmail.com

The Fanchor Story
by Mukesh Bhardwaj

ISBN : 978-93-6287-151-0
Collection of Short-Stories

Price : ₹ 350

Printed and bound in India at City Press, Delhi-110 095

Special thanks
Ashwini Bhatnagar, *Editor and Author*
Mrinal Vallari, *Research*
Publishers **Arun Maheshwari** *and* **Aditi Maheshwari Goyal**
Bandana Jha *and* **Gopal Jha**
Wife **Jaya**
Children **Deeksha-Mukul, Abhimanyu, Kartik**
and **Rohit**

Foreword

TV anchors are the face of journalism in popular imagination now.

They are the face that launch a thousand ships filled with narratives in the mid ocean of public beliefs and opinion, but are themselves navvies at the command of the bull horns.

The visibility of anchor-journalists, on the small screen and mini screens on mobile phones, have indeed made them popular media icons. The 'journalism icons' run their writ from glamorous ivory towers, but cater to the lowest common denominator in society — speaking the street language in a loud manner that begs immediate attention of people with a lot of free time at hand, and an attention span that needs constant booster shots.

They have succeeded by putting facts to sword, billeting the truth; by yelling, and name-calling while playing footsie with the moneyed and the influential. They are street smart, too — how else could they have turned 'national interest' into a revenue cataract?

Tragically, however, journalism ethics has given the dog a bad name, little realizing it is the tail that wags the dog and not the other way around. The faces on news TV channels are in fact those that have been carefully cultivated and crafted by visual media owners. They are, without doubt, flesh and blood people, many deeply grounded in the ethos of journalism, who made a choice to be mere puppets for the sake of four pieces of silver and fifteen minutes of fame.

Their dominance has come to pose an existential threat to real time, hands-on professional journalists.

When I first discussed this book with journalist, author and media academic Ashwini Bhatnagar, I had already penned six chapters. He did not agree TV anchors posed a real and substantial threat to journalism in India. Excellent journalistic work was being done in traditional media, he said, and on the web, the new carrier of news with an unmatched global reach.

I countered by saying that not only was the danger real but it had exacerbated into an existential crisis for journalism and journalists in India. Anchors, I said forcefully, were now the only journalist people know of; or even acknowledge as scribes. The rest, in print or in cyber space, did not matter. The anchor was its own Editor-in-Chief, TV presenter, reporter, analyst, commentator, etc. In other words, I said, it embodied all aspects of journalism in a single entity that had been packaged suitably to obliterate the role of professional journalists.

Yes, Ashwini Bhatnagar admitted, anchors and news channels were dominating public discourse, aided and abetted by a narrative- conscious regime; but, noise and untruths, he said, can never be journalism. It takes a lot more than a glib tongue, compromised sense of professional dignity, and a well- recognized face to do substantive journalism. The razzle dazzle of TV shows can be mistaken for journalism over a short term; and, when it is, it's a pyrrhic victory a victory that inflicts such a devastating toll on the victor that it is tantamount to defeat.

He, however, supported my idea of documenting the phenomenon of 'fanchors,' and the peddling of blatantly partisan views as news on prime time television. The phase had to be reported in full detail as a lesson for the future, he said.

Fanchors, I believe, started to get intensively cultivated like mushrooms in trays after Narendra Modi became Prime Minister in 2014. The first full majority Bhartiya Janta Party (BJP) government had reduced the ruling Congress to a political non entity in the Lok Sabha elections. The feat was repeated with better results in 2019. Modi was now all powerful — some even said invincible — in electoral battles. However, the 2024 Lok Sabha Elections results completely belied the notion. Modi was like any other politician who would compromise to any extent to stay in power. However, the mushrooms in the backyard of the power corridors had received plenty of water, manure and light during a decade of Modi rule because they were the essential nutrients for the daily political diet.

The Press has always been important for politicians. The Press, in turn, ensured its credibility by its accuracy, neutrality and impartiality. These were ethics of journalism which rarely needed formalisation through rules, regulations and guidelines. An editor, violating any one the cardinal principles of journalism, soon acquired a reputation that marred his career. Personal ideological agendas were therefore always left outside newsrooms and edit meetings.

This is not to say that editors or reporters did not have friendships with political leaders. In fact, friendships ran deep across the political spectrum. But they were rarely at play while newspaper pages or TV bulletins were being readied for release. Also, despite the difference of opinion between journalists and politicians, there was no enmity between them. Battle-lines were never drawn.

The practice continued till 2014. When Modi took over the reins of government, the BJP branded a certain set of journalists as the Khan Market Gang, Lutyens Media, or simply as presstitutes.

However, it was not that journalists did not matter to the BJP. They mattered, significantly. The only difference was it wanted complete control. It wanted to replace Free Press with Imprisoned Press, and Independent Journalists with Committed Journalists at the institutional level.

The Modi Sarkar went about the task with clinical precision. It dubbed individual journalists as presstitutes, libtards, etc. and muscled in on media owners. It had plenty of cash and influence to force compliance of its demand. Media owners wilted under the stare. "Then we have a few maliks (media owners) who have gone down on bended knees, so comfortable in their posture that it hurts if they stand up." Rajkamal Jha, Editor, The Indian Express defined the scenario in his unforgettable words at the Ram Nath Goenka Awards-2024. Fanchors are the children of this unholy matrimony.

The first news bulletin was aired on September 30, 1995, when a Malayalam channel Asianet broadcast it from a studio situated in the Philippines. Nationally, things had changed when former Prime Minister PV Narsimha Rao opened the doors for foreign investment in the country. But it took time for electronic news channels to set up shop.

Before their coming, TV news meant Doordarshan bulletins presented by a JV Raman or a Salma Sultan; the World This Week or The News Tonight by Prannoy Roy. But investment started pouring in soon enough and by 1998, all was set and within a few months Zee News entered Indian household with its first 24×7 news channel.

Prior to the entry of news channels, television was a source of entertainment airing vastly popular serials like Ramayana, Mahabharat, Buniyad, Hum Log, etc. Initially the news media was a welcome departure from sarkari information channel. It had news value minus entertainment. But in two decades, it has moved a full circle – it's mostly entertainment, news included.

Liberalisation had its own problems though. While, on one hand, it brought in sacks full of money for the news media to set up its glittering studios, demands of corporatisation of the media, on the other, needed a number of favours from the government. Quid pro quo slyly started to raise its head.

With time, regional and national politicians, business magnates, builders, and fly-by-night operators entered the fray with the sole motive of using the media to cozy up with the power elite. Enormous amounts of money was pumped into setting up news channels and well-known journalists were bought in steer their course to a government-media nexus.

The real problems for the electronic media however arose when competition between channels to attract advertising revenue peaked. Advertising is fully linked to TRP rankings. A small slide in ranking shaves off a big chunk of revenue. And, the government is the biggest source of revenue, directly and indirectly. The powerful ruling elite had to be kept in good humour, irrespective of the cost to ethics of the profession.

The race for survival, in fact, is the main reason why TV newsrooms have turned into laboratories of news creation, news generation and news curation.

There is the other side of television journalism, too. TV channels did in fact expose major scandals that caused considerable political flutter. However, the authenticity of sting operations soon took a beating when fake stings were aired for sake of TRPs.

Fanchors took over from there on. It was the easiest, cheapest route to keep a politically divided viewership engaged. It also had the backing of a very pleased ruling elite.

This short document on the state of Indian television since 2014, narrow focused especially on fanchors, is my attempt to put the prevailing situation on record. I have not detailed every episode of fanchors' journey. I have instead tried to give it a perspective with some examples. I hope readers will find the narration useful.

Contents

1

Anchorism

Our mythology is replete with captivating tales, one of which is the story of King Pondrak. He proclaimed himself to be Lord Krishna and, in an attempt to convince others, adorned himself in attire reminiscent of the deity. Consumed by his delusion, he adorned himself with a conch, peacock feather, and the Kaustubh gem. Flattery, a longstanding facet of our civilisation, led those with vested interests to go to great lengths to persuade him that he was indeed the true Krishna. However, like many characters in the Mahabharat, he met his ultimate downfall at the hands of Lord Krishna after crossing all bounds.

This narrative bears a striking resemblance to modern television anchors who have convinced themselves that they are the epitome of journalism. Holding forth on news often half-baked, underdeveloped, or even outright fake, they wield it like a divine discus, purporting themselves to be true journalists. Ironically, they face exposure not from a divine entity like Lord Krishna, but rather from the official spokespersons of the government, ruling party, or opposition on a daily basis. While impersonating government mouthpieces, they conveniently forget their expendability. Consequently, they are typically discarded into the trash can of history like paper napkins once they outlive their utility.

Yet, during their heyday, they fail to envision their eventual relegation to the annals of history. Enduring insults and humiliation from the ruling elite with a forced smile, they remain steadfast in serving the business interests of their masters. Consider the infamous exchange where Union Minister Smriti Irani subjected Aaj Tak anchor Sudhir Chaudhary to the humiliating question, "How did you feel when you went to jail?" Sudhir Chaudhary's visibly shaken demeanor during the live chat spoke volumes, highlighting the stark reality of their precarious position.

The viral video of this interview once again underscores the importance of respecting professional boundaries, a lesson that is repeatedly driven home. Every profession has its limits, and it is imperative that they are never breached.

In the late nineties, when we first tuned into the news on Doordarshan, the individuals delivering the news were commonly referred to as news readers, newscasters, or news presenters. They served as the vital link between journalism and the audience. The stories they relayed were meticulously prepared in the newsroom, where raw information from various sources was received, checked, written, and edited by the desk editors. Typically, news readers were not directly involved in journalistic endeavors; instead, they read out the prepared text due to their exceptional voice quality and precise pronunciation. The author is intimately familiar with this process, having served as a part-time news caster at All India Radio Chandigarh during his university days.

Back then, the news was presented simply as news, devoid of any emotional embellishments that have become commonplace today. There was no attempt to sensationalise the news or inject personal opinions or unnecessary rhetoric such as "why this" and "why that." Anchors refrained from intervening between the news and the facts, avoiding questioning the government's actions or inserting their own biases into the narrative.

Over time, the role of the anchor evolved, with the emergence of a blend of journalists and presenters, which gradually led to the term "anchor" becoming synonymous with journalism. However, in contemporary times, anchors find themselves in a precarious situation. Therefore, while upholding the sacred principles of journalism, the author suggests a new term to describe their role: "Anchorism."

The hallmark of 'Anchorism' lies in its perceived immunity from boundaries. Anchors often exceed their journalistic boundaries with impunity, prioritising sensationalism over responsible reporting, driven by the narratives dictated by their handlers. Consequently, they orbit around centers of power without restraint, blurring the lines between journalism and propaganda.

Another defining trait of 'Anchorism' is evident when interviewing government representatives. Anchors often adopt a congenial demeanor, selectively framing questions to favor the government's agenda while lambasting the opposition. Their questioning style exudes a veneer of democracy, even when receiving simplistic answers. This behavior strays far from the journalistic ethos, operating more as conduits for government messaging rather than independent watchdogs.

Following soft inquiries, 'Anchorism' shifts gears, assuming the role of government mouthpieces with aggressive fervor, mimicking official rhetoric with uncanny precision. Debates across channels echo identical narratives, rendering them indistinguishable. Even questioning the government's unfulfilled promises, such as the infamous pledge to retrieve black money from overseas accounts, is met with deflection and spin, obfuscating the truth from public scrutiny.

However, 'Anchorism' consistently fails to interrogate the source of funds or the whereabouts of the purported black money. Instead, their focus remains fixated on vilifying the opposition, amplifying partisan divides to a degree that viewers are left disillusioned with the media's integrity. This brand of pseudo-journalism not only undermines the public's ability to stay informed but also erodes trust in the media as a beacon of truth and accountability.

In the Indian education system, questioning holds a revered status, akin to worship. Rooted in the Vedas and Upanishads, questions form the bedrock of intellectual inquiry, akin to the sanctum sanctorum of a temple. Access to this realm demands honesty, integrity, and devotion. However, the sanctity of this space has been desecrated within the prime time newsrooms, where questions are pre-scripted, devoid of genuine curiosity.

The innate curiosity to question is intrinsic to human nature, especially evident in children's early inquiries. Parents play a pivotal role in nurturing this curiosity, fostering healthy mental development by patiently addressing each query. Conversely, responding with irritation stifles intellectual growth, mirroring the negative impact mirrored in the public sphere.

Modern journalism's essence lies in relentless inquiry, earning its status as the fourth pillar of democracy, independent and free from external influence. Yet, 'Anchorism' has subverted this ethos, inviting the ruling party's intrusion into journalistic sanctuaries. Oblivious to the government's propaganda machinery, they naively believed aligning with power would secure their position.

In pursuit of favor, 'Anchorism' espouses government narratives, vilifying the opposition without remorse. Ironically, they championed the two-thousand-rupee note, heralding it as a panacea for black money, only to remain silent when it was demonetised. Their complicity in perpetuating falsehoods undermines journalistic integrity, eroding public trust.

Now, within the hallowed halls of inquiry, power's spokespeople wield questions as weapons, inflicting wounds on those who dare challenge authority. This reversal of roles serves as a stark reminder of the consequences of forsaking journalistic principles for political expediency.

2

Farce of Fanchors

A stylishly dressed anchor sashayed into a colourfully decked up studio. A multi-camera set-up followed her every move as she walked across the floor. She stopped, and turned to face the camera, a slight smile playing on her lips.

"I am a journalist," she said emphatically to convince herself, before unrolling the rest of her belief system before the audience. "But this does not mean I don't feel strongly about various things. I have my own opinion on issues... and, I am not afraid of airing them." She paused; allowing it to sink in.

The candidness on her part was perhaps necessary. The long-standing host of the show had been fired recently for questioning the government's claims on doubling farm incomes. She was taking over the popular show on that day with her opinion firmly aligned with the official claims. She made it clear through the operative words in her opening statement — she was a "journalist," and, the fact of the matter was her opinion.

In other words, whatever the 'news', the 'view' on it was the defining quality of what constituted journalism on television. The anchor, at her maiden appearance on the new show, proceeded to castigate members of the political opposition even as she aligned herself, and her 'strong opinion,' with the ruling elite. She spoke loud and clear, silencing critics while bucking up the protagonists. At the end of the discussion, she blew the whistle on the critics, and announced the government as the winner. It was a very satisfying moment for the 'fanchor.' She had done her job admirably. Asked her questions splendidly "Aap Thakte Nahi ?" (Don't you get tired, ever ?).

Fanchor is a new word. It is a combo of two words – fan and anchor. An anchor of a show or a debate is usually someone who introduces the subject under discussion and calls the two opposing sides to debate their position. The anchor is impartial; it cuts in only to ensure the rules of the debate are not breached. It doesn't voice its opinion.

A fan, on the other hand, is deeply committed to a person or a cause embodied in a person. Its heart rules over its head; it sees, hears or speaks love and praise for its idol.

The two words have been combined to define the majority of television news anchors who have, over the last few years, discarded their neutrality for partisanship and given out views to justify or embellish news. They have incessantly argued against facts, thumbed down evidence and manufactured news angles for the sake of their 'strong opinion.'

Indian television news is therefore news for the fans, by the fans and of the fans. And, its anchors are 'fanchors— anchors who are fans first or fans who became anchors later; or whatever else as long as they are unabashedly partisan.

Television debates are not the only fan playground. Anchors have started to enact news sequences in the most dramatic manner with proper impact music and graphics running in the background. Fanchor is a new breed of people, nay journalists, who have come to occupy the centre stage in the electronic media space. The truth of the journalism practised by fanchors is bared in a simple question asked by a panellist during a TV debate: "Madam, would you clarify whether this question is from you or from the BJP?"

The question, and scores of others like it, many more acidic than this innocent query, define the 'for' and 'against' one-upmanship that has come to grip television since 2014. There have, of course, been several instances in the past —Emergency in 1975 and Babri Masjid demolition in 1992, to name the most prominent ones—, when the Press was vertically divided. But the criticism and support to each was never as virulent as it has been since 2014.

The media also never created noise over non issues with the deliberate purpose of deflecting public attention from an issue that was uncomfortable for the government. Orchestrated campaigns of diversion, vilification, red herrings or even simple trickery (clever video editing, etc.) have now become a large part of how fanchors create the news to suit their views. In fact, fake has become the new real on Indian TV.

Fake story as a TRP booster started much before politics came into play. One channel led from the front and its so-called stories on ghosts, witches, snake gods and tantric babas with miraculous cures were initial experiments to tap into audience curiosity on tall tales. It was soon followed by a host of other channels, including the market leader.

The specious plea given out by head honchos of these channels for prioritising fake content over real news was that it got them TRP ratings. We serve what the audience wants, they said to justify abandonment of editorial discretion and time-tested standard of fact-based journalism.

The dalliance with sorcery, demons, bogus mythology and religious fraud whetted the appetite of news channel owners who were previously battling revenue issues in the news television space. Bigger audience drew in bigger advertisers and the bottom lines of channels suddenly started to perk up.

The next 'innovation' was converting news into real-life drama. The numero uno of Indian news channels pioneered it to a large extent when it broadcast uninterrupted live coverage of the rescue of a boy named Prince who was trapped in a bore-well in Haryana. Even small incidents, thereafter, were given the make-over of drama. The mantra was overkill is better than no kill at all.

Each human story was thereafter grabbed with both hands and wringed mercilessly for its drama and emotion. Most times, drama was staged for the cameras and reported as on-the-spot live coverage. Editors and producers, all professional journalists, specifically instructed reporters to 'arrange' scenes to liven up routine stories.

The unprofessional greed to get provocative bytes and emotion–laced visuals converted television news reporting into crude theatrics in which news stories had no news; they were rather hurriedly made up tales designed to hook the viewer for the next 90 seconds. The dictum — news is where the money is — began to unfold its hydra-headed form across news channels in India.

In fact, much before 2014, channels had already covered themselves with the inglorious practise of peddling narratives which went against the very grain of journalistic ethics and professional conduct. A news story was commissioned not on the basis of its journalistic merit but on the grounds whether it will 'sell or not sell.' Hindi television channels led all other language channels in trivialising news and prioritising bogus content.

The stage had therefore been set by journalists, abdicating

their professional responsibilities in lieu of fatter pay packets, for politicians to occupy at their convenience; and, on their terms.

Channel owners, after their profitable dalliance with non-political fakery, were only too pleased to add the lucrative political client to their already diversified 'news portfolio.' The tantric babas performing Shani bhagwan ki aarti were replaced by netas in spotless whites promising divine deliverance from the scourge of all social, political and economic ills.

Television returned to Breaking News, but in a different avatar. The race to `Break News` and beat rivals by milliseconds ensured speed minus accuracy. Even a rumour triggered a news break race.

During the Covid-19 pandemic, thousands of migrant workers rushed to the Bandra station in Mumbai after one channel aired a rumour (as their break) that special trains had been deployed to take workers home. The melee at the site was a potential Covid super spreader event.

In another instance, the president of Defence Colony Resident Welfare Association, New Delhi, was declared to have succumbed to coronavirus whereas he was hale and hearty. The president reacted to the story via social media thus, "I am president of Defence Colony Welfare Association and alive as of now. Are you reading my near future? Idiots, wake up."

Similarly, a channel, whose owner is a leading politician, was forced to apologize for carrying fake news regarding coronavirus patients. The fakery was exposed by fact checkers on social media.

A leading Hindi poet shared a Facebook post of one Manika Mohini of Noida who narrated her ordeal when she wanted to get herself tested for Covid. She rushed from pillar to post — private to government hospitals, district administration to health authorities — but none was willing to administer her the test. "Finally, when after our rigorous persuasion, I was tested and found positive, I, along with my husband, reached a dirty, dilapidated building listed as an isolation centre. My husband too was asked to be quarantined though he showed no symptoms and my 15-month old daughter was at home alone... We had to virtually snatch our report that was negative, begging them to release us and with great effort and after a lot of trouble were given an ambulance that first left us on road and then took us home at 1 a.m." read the Facebook post.

The most important portion of the post was: "We had been seeing on TV channels how flawlessly the state government was working on this front and the state was providing five-star facilities to the patients treating them with utmost care whereas we witnessed first-hand that it was exactly the opposite to its claim. So much so that nobody at the so-called isolation centre was wearing protective gear...there was no soap or sanitiser for cleaning our hands."

The overall government response to the Covid crisis worried renowned writer and analyst Yuval Noah Harari, who wrote, "People need to trust science, to trust public authorities, and to trust the media. Over the past few years, irresponsible politicians have deliberately undermined trust in science, in public authorities and in the media. Now these same irresponsible politicians might be tempted to take the high road to authoritarianism, arguing that you just cannot trust the public to do right things. Normally, trust that has been eroded for years cannot be rebuilt overnight. But these are not normal time."

The powers-that-be, however, will not have the truth; they just wanted their own version of truth to be echoed by the people and the media. It, in many ways, made it mandatory for people to love the government in order to affirm their love for the country. Institutions too, — the executive, legislature, judiciary, and the fourth estate — had to love the government first and foremost if they did not want to be pressurised or slurred into submission. A number of them who dillydallied were labelled anti-national, traitors, communists, or, in worst cases, Pakis. Dissent, in short, was anti-national, and, therefore, had to be purged ruthlessly.

Ironically, TV channels celebrated the onslaughts calling them 'master strokes' played by the ruling dispensation. When the country was facing acute financial crisis following demonetisation and GST in the wake of a recession, news channels were busy running prime time debates on Pakistan's economy! They compared vegetable prices in the two countries to affirm Modi government's astute economics. Tomatoes were priced between Rs 60 and Rs 80 per kg India, they trumpeted, while the price in Pakistan was Rs 200 per kg.

Harari, in his long article, also drew the attention of the readers on how governments were chasing people online, not to link them with welfare measures but to create a surveillance regime. He writes, "Instead of building a surveillance regime, it is not too late to rebuild people's trust in science, in public authorities and in the media. We should definitely make use of news technologies too, but these should empower citizens. I am all in favour of monitoring my body temperature and blood pressure, but that data should not be used to create an all-powerful government. Rather, that data should enable me to make more informed personal choices, and also to hold government accountable for its decision."

With the introduction of Adhaar card, the unique identification for all the Indians, the government took every step to establish a surveillance regime throwing all objections to it to the winds. The measures suddenly brought George Orwell and his book 1984 into discussion and it seemed that he had foreseen the eventuality decades ago.

Even during Corona times, the government found an opportunity to further consolidate its surveillance on common people when it reportedly ordered chemists to keep track of individual medical prescriptions.

In the 1990s, media tycoon Rupert Murdoch transformed journalism into a glamorous apparition. After three decades, the apparition has solidly dented journalism. A glaring example, again from the time of the pandemic, was the case of the Tablighi Jamat congregation and allegations of it being the super spreader of the deadly virus. Nearly 2000 people were 'found', it was said, under one roof in the heart of New Delhi. Nobody had surprisingly noticed the gathering before the news broke.

Suddenly, TV screens exploded with images of the Jamaat meet and concerns about their role in the spread of the virus. The incident was hyped to the maximum when Ajit Doval, National Security Adviser of the Modi Government, personally visited Jamaat headquarters in Nizammudin locality to persuade the members to disperse. The word out on the streets, and on TV debates, was that Muslims were deliberately spreading Covid -19, even when there was no evidence to support the charge. All channels went into a frenzy to connect the Muslim gathering into an act of Islamic terrorism.

Along with the Jamaat, another breaking news charade was the Prime Minister's interviews on several channels by specially selected journalists asking specially supplied questions from him. It became a set pattern for news channels to only mouth questions given out to them and smile gratefully at the answers dished out by the PM. The dumbing down of news channel journalists was complete when actor Akshay Kumar interviewed Modi and asked him the most pertinent question ever asked in television history: "Aap aam kaise khate hain? Kaat kar ya choos kar? (How do you eat mangoes? Do you cut and slice them or eat them whole)".

The force of such interviews reached its crescendo on the eve of first phase of the 2024 Lok Sabha polls. Prime Minister Narendra Modi wrote on his X handle, "Do read my interview with @newsweek, in which I have shared my thoughts on various issues, both domestic and international.
newsweek.com/2024/04/19".

A US based writer and columnist Edward Luce was quick to retort , "This is not an interview. It's stenography."

It was also the time when one-sided press conferences became the norm. Ministers addressed the media in a soliloquy and walked out. No questions were allowed to be asked. The classic example was the Prime Minister himself; who, after repeated attacks from Opposition parties for not holding a press conference during his first tenure, walked in with BJP president Amit Shah at a press gathering and declared, "I am a disciplined soldier of the party; the president will answer questions." News channels applauded Modi's statement instead of questioning his reluctance to speak with the Press.

Professor Chatman of UC Berkeley once observed, "There is a U-shape to the effect of flattery: effective up to a certain point, but beyond that it would be too obvious and therefore counter-productive." News channels in India, however, continued to believe otherwise. They would rather praise the `Supreme Leader` unquestioningly than question what the praise was all about.

3

Brazen Bias

"Aap maryada ka dhyan rakhen (Please remember your limits). I give you some time to apologise for what you have said. I hope after we return from the break, you will not only withdraw your words but would also apologise for them," stammered a visibly shaken anchor on a national news channel after Congress spokesperson Rajiv Tyagi called him a `dalal` (pimp).

``No, my dear friend, I will not repeat my words but if you so insist let me tell you that you are a `dalal patrakar`," fumed Tyagi, who, prior to this observation, said "We (the Congress) allowed 500 channels because of which `dalals` like you (the anchor) became journalists." The country has more than 800 channels now. Half of them are news channels.

There is another scenario in which a channel head and lead anchor of an aggressively right-tilted channel dared the Chief Minister, Home Minister, Police Chief and the main spokesperson of the ruling party of a state to sit down for an interview with him. Pat came the reply, ``Interviews are given to journalists and not to the 'dalals.'

This anchor had earlier been snubbed by a number of leaders and panellists on his debates when he did not allow them to speak. ``Why do you even call us when you have to go on a marathon with your own voice?" an incensed panellist wondered on his show.

But the pique did not move the channel to tone down its voice. A reporter of the channel uttered expletives on camera, and a panellist, introduced as a retired General and top defence commentator, hurled profanities during a live chat.

There were no exceptions when it came to being snubbed on screen. Former Indian Cricket captain Saurav Ganguly took pot-shots at a TV news veteran during a live chat. He said, "You have recently been scolded by the former President of India," he said with a smirk. The former President Pranab Mukherjee had snubbed the anchor, saying, ``Don't forget you are interviewing the former President of the country. There is a basic courtesy." The anchor had no choice but to apologise.

The best, however, came from Vikas Singh, advocate of Sushant Singh Rajput, when the channel tried to corner him on the question of media trial. The anchor said it seems media wants to settle this case on TV screens. Vikas Singh retorted, ``If you think so, then why this interview? You have invited me to speak to you. I do not want this." He removed his lapel mike and left; leaving the anchor looking at an empty chair.

As if this was not enough, a channel, while covering the Sushant Singh Rajput murder case, knocked at the bedroom door of the parents of an accused in the alleged drugs case. The reporter was thrown out, also pushed down the stairs, by the family. Barging into bedrooms or breaking into the Intensive Care Unit (ICU) of a hospital with impunity was the new normal for news channels. The idea was to create drama, however sordid and disgusting. The daily dose at evening debates became representative of so- called electronic media journalism. It thrived on slanderous sensationalism and frightening jingoism.

The 2014 general election saw India acquiring its first full majority non-Congress government under Prime Minister Narendra Modi. Whenever required by the powerful, news media became a deflecting agent and tried to mislead people on major issues. It raised the national flag regularly and urged citizens to follow the state's diktats for the sake of the country.

BJP spokesperson Sambit Patra, who lost Lok Sabha elections from Bhubaneshwar, took to typical whataboutery while reacting to The Hindu story regarding Chinese occupation of 1000 square kilometres of Indian territory, "Will you believe a reporter or the Prime Minister of the country?," he asked arching his eye brows.

The response came when his counterpart tried to corner him on the government claims that not even an inch of land had been captured by the Chinese during the most furious border clash since 1967. The Hindu had carried a story that a large chunk of land was seized by China. It was still under its possession. Twenty Indian soldiers had been killed in a hand- to- hand combat on borders of Ladakh during a bloody clash over it. The incident had shaken up the country that was already battling the Covid-19 pandemic.

On September 7, 2020, shots were fired at the Line of Actual Control (LAC) on eastern Ladakh border after a gap of 45 years. Tensions were high between both the countries, and, had it not been for Rhea Chakarborty and Kangana Ranaut, channels would have been flexing their muscles at China. But, celebrity attraction scored over `nationalistic bravado` for gaining TRPs.

Or, they were told to avoid mention of the border situation and divert viewer attention to a celebrity issue. Rajput's death was a convenient 'news peg' to shift from the more pressing issues before the country.

In fact, the electronic media was unabashedly used to extol the virtues and masculinity of the Sarkar and to sensationalise a simple story of suicide (Sushant Singh Rajput case). It was obviously not serious journalism focused on serious issues. So, whenever news channels took a break from their prime duty of sycophancy, they preferred to set up a stage that would put a fish market to shame.

While in Times Now, Arnab Goswami cobbled a trend wherein the anchor ruled the show. He had the licence to humiliate or insult the panellists. Other channels quickly aped him. A number of journalists, opinion makers and general viewers called the NDTV India bold and fearless, but the channel too, knowingly or unknowingly, followed the trait of cursing all other channels by labelling them Godi (pro Modi) media.

Though NDTV India never named any particular anchor, it generally berated other channels in a self-righteous arrogant tone. The nationalist anchors, on thc other hand, were noisy and deeply partisan. They threw journalistic neutrality to the winds and took a strong stand in favour of the Right brigade. Ironically, this vital platform that could have played a major constructive role in a democratic set-up like India became an auditorium where actors appeared in the garb of anchors and declared their unabashed allegiance to the powers that be.

Media houses, in fact, adopted a dubious approach to earn the pleasure of Sarkar. The slant in their various publications was different to the governments at state and central level. For instance, ABP News, owned by the Anand Bazar Patrika group, toed the central government line to such an extent that it was accused of shunting out its editors and two prime time anchors at the behest of the Modi Government.

Their English daily, The Telegraph, published from Kolkata, however, took a stinging approach towards the Modi Government and rarely missed an occasion to hit at the Prime Minister directly.

Barring NDTV that was accused of toeing anti- government line, almost all other channels became a puppet show. They blindly endorsed every decision of the government, right from demonetisation to its approach towards tackling the Covid-19 crisis. Though government actions drowned the economy, anchors were busy demonising actress Rhea Chakarborty as if she was some sort of mafia or a drug lord. Anchors violently defended state decisions as if they were their own and blatantly trumpeted exaggerated state claims. Ministers appeared on their shows and snubbed them if they found their questions inconvenient.

This was the time indeed of fluffy staged interviews where ingratiating anchors bent backwards and felt proud on being embarrassed by their conduct. No wonder under the circumstances the Opposition called journalists conducting these interviews with a pre-decided questionnaire in hand 'pliable.'

Never before 2014, television functioned as the mouthpiece of a certain party, and, then later, of a certain government, and, finally, of a certain individual. It became difficult to differentiate between an anchor and the ruling party spokesperson. On one such occasion, a spokesperson for Tablighi Jamat asked a cantankerous and noisy anchor of the No 1 channel, ``This question is from your side or from the BJP?" They later had a showdown during the debate.

The 24/7 television revolutionized the presentation of news that hardly stuck to its basic principles of representing hard facts and non-partisanship. Instead, it became highly speculative and starkly opinionated presentation of half-truths. On a number of occasions, news seemed a lousy attempt at distracting the viewers from real issues of public concern.

The division between the media and respective state governments became so evident that the Maharashtra Vidhan Sabha brought a privilege motion against Arnab Goswami for his attack on the Chief Minister and other leaders. Some newspapers carried this story on September 9, 2020, though majority of the newspapers avoided it. The next day, Indian Express carried an item that three persons, including two journalists with the Republic Media Network, had been arrested on September 9 for allegedly trespassing Maharashtra Chief Minister Uddhav Thakre's farmhouse at Khalapur in Raigad district. The Republic TV called it an illegal custody to silence the Channel. The arrested persons were following a journalistic lead in an investigative assignment, it claimed.

Journalism took the backseat in news channels. Personal vendetta, due to collusion between the Union government and media houses, became the measure to decide the slant of the TV coverage of every event happening in the state or country. The confrontation between the Republic Media Network and Maharashtra Government and the rift between Kangana Ranaut and Maharashtra Government were brazen examples of electronic media coverage under the rule of Sarkar. Unfortunately, neither the Press Council of India or the Editors Guild of India or any news broadcasting body came forward to stem the rot.

4

Investigator, Prosecutor, Judge

"It is in the court of law where every evidence produced by the police is evaluated and where it may be contested. Others cannot usurp the role of police and create a false narrative. The court of law is the correct forum for this purpose. Investigation is judged on the basis of evidence and not perception," S. N. Srivastava, Commissioner of Police, Delhi, said in an interview to The Hindu, on October 25, 2020.

The comment was made while responding to a question on February, 2020, riots in North East Delhi which claimed 50 lives. The reference was to the riots but it was an adequate observation on the media that had taken up the role of investigator, prosecutor and judge upon itself unilaterally. TV anchors had passed the guilty verdict on certain individuals in various criminal cases.

Its worst face was seen in the actor Sushant Singh death case in which Republic TV wanted a case of murder registered. A humiliating mashup showing an anchor crying for a case under Section 302, CrPC however failed to deter the network. It continued the campaign relentlessly, even as CBI concluded it was case of suicide.

The channel also started a campaign hashtag #Arrest Rhea on Twitter. The Bombay High Court asked Republic TV,

"Why should anyone be arrested for a case that is still under investigation? And, how does such a demand fall under the category of investigative journalism?" The court also expressed its astonishment that if the channel was to convict people in a case that was under probe, what will the courts do?

The High Court made a scathing commentary on electronic journalism. It asked Republic TV that a case (Sushant Singh Rajput suicide case) was being investigated for a homicide or a suicide, but the channel was claiming it to be a murder. A division bench of Justice Dipankar Gupta and Justice GS Kulkarni asked the channel, ``If you become investigator, prosecutor and the judge, what is the use of us?" It went further, pushing the channel to the wall, "If you are so interested in unearthing the truth, you should have looked at the CrPC! Ignorance of law is no excuse."

But a number of channels tilted the case with impunity as per their perception in their effort to grab TRPs in utter disregard to the individual freedom and privacy of the parties concerned. Media trial had been in focus in a few of other cases also, including the Jessica Lall, Arushi Talwar and Nitish Katara murder case, but it came under sharp scrutiny in the Sushant Singh case in which it crossed all limits and took so-called investigative journalism to a new low.

Similarly, TV reporters sent from Delhi to cover the Hathras rape-murder case indulged in video activism and an ABP reporter performed a sit- in in the village of the victim after the police stopped her from going to the victim's house. She confronted the police and administrative officers and started a dharna at the spot. Little did she know that the personnel posted at the spot were merely doing their duty, and it would have invited disciplinary action had they allowed her to reach the spot. She neither seemed aware of this nor did the seniors at her office tried to tell her that the drama might get eyeballs and TRPs but it won't lead her to the victim's home. For this, she had to knock at a different door.

In a majority of cases involving a celebrity, anchors claimed information from police sources as their own investigation, and the `khulasa`, (expose) continued for days and weeks. Depending on the celebrity quotient of the person, the so-called exposes were labelled `Maha Khulasa`, `Bada Khulasa,' and sometimes `Sub se bada Khulasa.'

The reporters on 'ground zero,' as the anchors claimed, relayed information breathlessly so as to make it more and more dramatic. Depending upon the stature of the celebrity, they would first inject curiosity in the minds of the general public through a systematic release of speculative and imaginative dose of information; and then interpret it in a thousand ways while Sherlock Homes squirmed in his grave.

A joke on social media said that North Korea dictator Kim Yong Un watched Indian television channels to get information on his future strategy.

If the channel bosses felt that the 'story' was very important, they deputed their prime time anchor to the spot. The anchor would jump into a boat to cover a flood or wear a natty suit matching the personal protective equipment (PPE) kit with gum shoes while anchoring the show, or borrow Army fatigues while reporting on Indo-China border crisis.

In a mockery of visual journalism, star anchors gave poor performances as actors but they were accepted by viewers who confused them with journalists.

In fact, when responsibility will be fixed for giving journalism a bad name, it will primarily rest with television anchors. They dramatised investigations in the worst possible way.

Sting operations met with some success and became popular during the early days of TV news but they soon lost their sting as they failed judicial scrutiny. A new channel, launched with great fanfare and which was reportedly patronised by some ruling party leaders, ran a sting operation on Babri Masjid demolition case but no one was convinced about its authenticity.

Another channel, launched by a journalist having close ties with the BJP, organised a sting that had everything but sting. It was the same channel that was launched by Prime Minister Narendra Modi where he made an observation that the team running the show was full of journalists who abused him. The video clip had gone viral. A book written by its promoter was also released by RSS chief Mohan Bhagwat and the function was attended by then BJP chief Amit Shah and the then Home Minister Rajnath Singh.

All channels, in fact, wanted to prove that they were the first to report on a development even as news agency clip ran simultaneously on their screens. Every other story was `Exclusive`, `Maha Exclusive`, Super Exclusive` and it became 'Super Explosive' after senior journalist Rajdeep Sardesai interviewed actress Rhea Chakarborty, who was booked by Patna Police in an abetment to suicide case on the complaint of K.K. Rajput, father of actor Sushant Singh Rajput.

The anchors tried people as accused in their own on screen courts where certain panellists also joined them in the tirade. TV channels categorised their panellist as `for` and `against` or `ke sath` and `ke khilaf. They ran online polls to decide whether the accused was innocent or guilty. This happened in case of Arushi Murder case, Jessica Lall Murder case, and Sushant Singh suicide case.

The fake sting operation of a Delhi teacher was still fresh in the mind of the people of the country. It destroyed an innocent life. This sting appeared on the same channel that 'discovered' a tracking chip in the new Rs 2000 note issued by the Modi government during the period of demonetisation. According to this anchor, intelligence agencies could unearth black money even if it was buried deep under the earth.

In the mid of the controversy over the objectionable coverage of the Sushant Singh Rajput case, and when a number of former anchors and journalists picked up their pen to slam it, there came a very significant observation from the Delhi High Court on Congress leader Shashi Tharoor's interim plea to restrain the Republic TV from levelling allegations over an ongoing trial of his wife Sunanda Pushkar's death. Pushkar was found dead in a five-star hotel in the capital on January 17, 2014.

Justice Mukta Gupta reminded channel's anchor Arnab Goswami of his undertaking to exercise restraint while reporting on Pushkar's death, submitted to the court earlier. Justice Gupta also questioned Goswami's claim that it was a murder while the charge sheet said that it was a case of abetment to suicide. ``Were you (Goswami) at the spot? Are you an eye witness? You must respect the sanctity of an ongoing investigation," said the Judge.

It was not the only instance wherein anchors judged the case on their own. The tone and tenor of the Rajput case too was the same where anchors tried to present it first as an abetment to suicide, and then as a murder. But anchors hardly learned. Days before this observation, and when the case was under judicial scrutiny, the anchor minced no words when he said on his channel, ``Rhea Chakarborty killed or not killed SSR but she definitely had a role in his murder."

The Rajput case helped Republic TV to dethrone Aaj Tak from its more than two decades long stay at the No 1 position. It continued its marathon coverage for nearly a month. This led to a confrontation between the two channels. Goswami screamed, ``Sun lo Aaj Tak walo," and, in turn, India Today TV called it `Banana Republic` channel.

Zee TV that had slipped on the TRP ratings tried to remind other channels of maryada, but, when it did not help, it too came out with a sort of 'maha exclusive' video clip in which Rhea was shown smoking with SSR and his friends. This was presented as if they were smoking marijuana.

An astrologer, Indu Prakash on India TV, called Rajput's death 'shahadat' (martyrdom) and launched his own investigation during his daily astrological capsule. Every morning, Indu Prakash told the viewers how the case will progress. His daily forecast was based on his reading of planetary movement. Prakash once announced that a big twist would happen in the SSR case with the entry of a big shot but when it did not happen, he started predicting about Kangana Ranaut case the next day.

Clearly, television channels were out to grind their own axe while reporting the death of Rajput. The ruling BJP found in it an opportunity to corner the Aghadi Government of Udhav Thakre in Maharashtra. Kangana Ranaut directly took on Thakre and dared him on Twitter after the Bombay Municipal Corporation dismantled illegal construction in her office building.

She compared him with Mughal King Babar, and described her own office as 'temple' which she said will be rebuilt.

The Shiv Sena was already on the offensive over her utterances regarding Thakre and the party. In its typical style,

Shiv Sena dared Kangana to come back to Mumbai which she promptly accepted and announced a date. Kangana reached Mumbai flanked by a dozen security personnel as the Centre Government gave her Y plus security in view of the threat. By the evening of September 10, 2020, a day after Kangana reached Mumbai, her parents joined the BJP and thanked Prime Minister Narendra Modi and Home Minister Amit Shah for their support to their daughter.

It was matter of time that Kangana Started chanting 'Jai Shri Ram' louder than even the committed BJP workers and finally got ticket as the BJP candidate in her home constituency Mandi in Himachal Pradesh.

The Rajput case, which initially seemed a case of suicide, witnessed a number of TV news story-telling twists, including abetment to suicide, nepotism in Bollywood, murder, drug cartel and, finally, political vendetta. All these angles were investigated, judged and decided by none other than the anchors with their unending rhetorical conclusions.

Amid this cacophony where every programme and its anchor had its own opinion about the case, the public awaited anxiously for them to ask relevant questions. The real issue of the death of the actor was forgotten and the entire case took a political turn where the right wing was seen strongly behind Kangana. A fake trial was on.

After Rhea Chakarborty's fake media trial, senior editor Shekhar Gupta tweeted, ``Rhea is being subjected to a brutal, medieval witch-hunt. Doubly tragic that a large section of TV media is part of the mob inquisition. Next, they would want her burnt at the stake. Shame on us, India...``

The coverage of the case was enough for the judiciary to ask whether there was a regulatory body for the electronic media. The Bombay High Court expressed its surprise that there were no statutory provisions for the electronic media. The court made the observation while hearing two public interest litigations alleging that the media was showing Bombay police in a bad light.

"We are surprised to find there is no state control over electronic media," the Bench comprising Chief Justice Dipankar Dutta and Justice GS Kulkarni noted. "This body (News Broadcasting Standards Authority) has no teeth at all is our prima facie view," the Scroll.in reported on September 12, 2020.

Additional Solicitor General Anil Singh, who represented the Centre, told the bench that the Press Council of India was a statutory body under the Press Council Act, 1978, while the National Broadcasters Association was a 'self-regulatory' body for news channels. It was so because the electronic media demanded freedom equivalent to print and other forms of media.

In the heat of this debate, an electronic channel Sudarshan News started a series titled `Bindaas Bol` aimed at highlighting what it called UPSC Jihad. The channel aired fragments of this programme. In the meantime, a petition was filed in Supreme Court for pre-telecast ban on the show. The channel did extensive promos for the programme which were anchored by its editor Suresh Chavhanke. It not only accused that the Muslims were, in a systematic way, infiltrating country's elite service but also raised certain questions about funding and motives of the Zakat Foundation.

The Supreme Court took strong objection to the show and minced no words while castigating the intent of the programme to harm the minority community. It said there was a need to send a message to the media that it cannot target a religious minority. Justice KM Thomas observed, "These attacks will marginalise people who want to come to the mainstream." Going further, he also said, "You may end up driving them into the wrong hands. Every community strives to have a voice in bureaucracy. What is wrong in that?"

Justice DY Chandrachud, while making an important observation in the case, regretted the role of regulatory bodies. The court seemed perturbed about the fact that the media lacked a self- regulatory mechanism, and, had it been there, the courts would not have intervened in the matter. The observation also missed state provisions to regulate such a matter. He said, ``A pre telecast injunction is like a nuclear missile. The court would not have intervened had the government, and regulatory bodies had a viable mechanism for self- regulation."

Justice Chandrachud's words created a vivid picture of the horrible programme that had come under severe attack from various quarters for its divisive nature. He wrote, ``Flames come up on the screen, bearded people in skull caps and the colour green are featured when a reference to a Muslim is made in the show. Every time you refer to the UPSC, you show ISIS and jihad." He also said, "We are very conscious of the fact that pre-publication, pre-telecast ban by us is a matter of extreme recourse. We do not do it easily." The court put a restrain on the show.

Sudarshan TV, during the course of the hearing, tried to make a case for a fact- based journalistic investigation, but it got a rap from the court. But, despite the court's displeasure, other channels too were doing the same thing. Evening debates were less debate and more agenda-setting for the ruling party. Topics were picked with a slanted tagline and invariably one would hear the panellists telling the anchor, "Please don't put your words in my mouth."

Anchors asked leading questions and interrupted the panellist if any of them made an attempt to say something against their own pre-set agenda. It was a time of blatantly biased journalism where no sane voice was heard.

Every discussion challenged the patriotism of the panellists. `Nation wants to know` transformed into `Poochhta hai Bharat`. On a number of occasions, it was a tough task to distinguish between the anchor and the official spokesman of the ruling party.

And, when Republic TV and Aaj Tak went into a tough battle over TRPs after Arnab pipped Aaj Tak from No 1 slot, Aaj Tak was quick to copy the title Poochta hai Bharat and add its own twist to it —Poochhta hai Aaj Tak. Accusations were thrown at each other, and, at one stage, one channel charged another channel with manipulating the Hathras victim's family for the sake of TRP. It was horrible to see the channels vertically divided over the sensitive issue of gang rape and murder.

A majority of channels though were with the family of the victim and left no stone unturned to push the UP administration to the wall to bring the voice of the family to the fore. In the midst of the crowd, one 'rashtravadi' (nationalist) channel tried to find chinks in the statements of the victim's family by unabashedly justifying the attitude of the UP government.

The Hathras issue however gave Rahul Gandhi an opportunity to come out shining as a political leader. Under severe pressure from the media and public, the Sarkar had to bite the dust and allow Rahul Gandhi to visit the victim's family. A day before, he had been halted by the police in Noida itself.

It was a million dollar question whether anchors were asked to do the slanted oratory or it came from their own volition. Remember that 2014-2024 period was called, 'Bhakti kaal of politics.' The titles of the programmes smacked of nationalistic bravado. Sample a few — Matrabhoomi, Rashtra ke Naam, Desh pe Qurban, Bharat ki Baat, Vande Matram etc. They should have been embarrassed about them but they were actually proud!

Hence, whenever anchors were dared on live debates about their partisan presentations, they defended it and hurled counter charges on the questioning panellists.

5

Issues of Choice

Even during the severe Covid-19 crisis, the great Indian media divide continued unabated. Charges were freely levied by one group at the other over their ethical positioning in this medical emergency. Believers were out with their naked swords to cut down the atheists, and vice versa.

The lynching of two ascetics and their driver at Palghar in Maharashtra gave them an opportunity to settle scores. The entire lot of TV anchor-bhakts, instead of pushing the central government to intervene or holding the prevalent religious hatred responsible for it, blasted Left liberal politicians for their 'indulgence' towards anti-national, anti-Hindu elements. Leading journalists, known for their liberal approach, were taunted for their silence over the issue.

Republic TV anchor Arnab Goswami, in his usual frenzied manner, resigned from the membership of Editors' Guild of India accusing it of hypocrisy. He also unleashed his anger and used certain unkind words about the then Guild president and veteran journalist Shekhar Gupta during the cacophony of his show. He said, "Shekhar Gupta, you hear it from me. Whatever has been remaining of the credibility of the Editors' Guild of India has been destroyed by the abject silence on a series of fake news. It has become a self-serving organisation.

I have been a member of the Editors' Guild for a long time. I, hereby, resign for absolute compromise of editorial ethics."

Though the apparent reason behind the incident was mistaken identity, Goswami was not convinced. It was not a case of mistaken identity, he claimed, and said that the intentions behind the incident were not 'clear.' He was booked by the police on charges of spreading communal hatred.

The Mumbai police took him into custody for interrogation which continued for nearly twelve hours. While his channel cried foul, it did not find support in any of the other news channels. A section of media, BJP leaders and other activists rallied behind Arnab Goswami and cited the example of NDTV's Ravish Kumar. The troll army alleged on social media that Kumar was biased and against Modi government but he had not been booked for his criticism.

Goswami, on the other hand, had been made a target by Maharashtra government. The Congress, a part of the ruling combine with its determining influence, was blamed for the 'unlawful' hounding of the anchor.

However, this was not the first time that the journalists were washing their dirty laundry in public. Since 2014, after the BJP came to power under Prime Minister Narendra Modi, a section of the media had been branded as `Godi media (Pro Modi)`. The other section was quickly labelled as `Virodhi media` (Anti Modi). The divide between Modi and Virodhi was crystal clear. Under such circumstances, journalism took a back seat as the rivals clashed over petty issues.

If this was not enough, in the heat of the moment, renowned historian Ram Chandra Guha too entered the fray. He announced that he will not write for The Hindustan Times because it had censored his column `Past and Present`. The article was on Modi's favourite Central Vista project in the heart of the national capital Delhi. Guha's words were testimony to how the media organisations were behaving when Modi was in power.

He said, "For print and online readers, my regular Past and Present column in The Hindustan Times –for this Sunday's issue I had written on the folly and vanity of the Central Vista project." Then he straightaway accused the newspaper management of censoring his piece. He said, "The editors were happy to publish the piece. I was given the option of junking this piece and continuing the column. I have chosen to stop writing for them altogether." There was a subtle charge that the editors were overruled by the management.

Later, the article was carried in full by web portal, The Wire. The first part of the article included verbatim references from a piece written by Alpana Kishore published on the website Newslaundry that challenged the government's decision to redevelop Central Vista on priority, especially the key element, the provision for a grand new house for the Prime Minister on Rajpath. "Such self-indulgence may be common in dictatorships, but was inappropriate for a Republic."

Slamming the project in the harshest possible words, she wrote, `The biggest irony remains that a Prime Minister from the humblest of backgrounds should yearn for a house on Rajpath, no less, to endorse his vision of personal greatness and legacy. Would Emmanuel Macron demand and, more importantly, get a house on the Champs Elyee's? Can even Trump order himself a second home on the Mall?"

Her sarcasm got sharper as the article progressed. She remarked, "It brings back embarrassing memories of his name-embroidered on Rs 10 lakh suit, only this time the vanity will beat the taxpayer's expense."

Guha, in his piece, rubbed salt into the yet festering wound of this article when he wrote, "The Modi government's redesign of New Delhi brings to mind not so much living Communist autocrats as it does some dead African despots. It is sort of vanity project, designed to perpetuate the ruler's immortality, that Felix Houphouet-Boigny of Ivory Coast and Jean Bedel Bokassa of the Central African Republic once inflicted on their own countries."

He wanted this project to be shelved because of the Covid-19 crisis faced by the government at hand. "It will be at least a year – probably longer – before the economy can begin to fitfully recover. The restoration of social fabric may take even longer. Altogether, the country may take at least five, more likely ten, years before it can return to where it was before Covid– 19 came to our shores."

His language was seething and laced with sarcasm. "In his speeches to the nation since the pandemic broke, the Prime Minister has repeatedly asked Indians to sacrifice – sacrifice their time, their jobs, their lifestyles, their human and cultural tendency to be gregarious. Now citizens must ask the Prime Minister to sacrifice something for the nation as well. His project to redesign Central Vista was always controversial. It is now absolutely untenable. He should drop it."

This was the most crucial juncture for the commentators. It was a never- before kind of situation since Modi took over in 2014 that a freelance writer of Guha's stature stood up for himself and his views. A slight slant in his story would have saved his piece but he preferred freedom of his expression over a meek surrender.

Meanwhile, another strong voice of dissent Pratap Bhanu Mehta carried on his column though the usual sting against the ruling elite went missing. Sample this: "But we are in an era of new nationalism. It is not important that the real problems in agriculture be solved. It is more important that our Supreme Representative not be seen to bend. When new nationalism requires everyone else to show they have no spine, one spine must remain firm, even if the country breaks." (Indian Express February 6, 2021)

Now everybody knew who he had referred to as Supreme Representative. But he had stopped short of writing the name. Save your job. Save your Column. Depends whether you are in a job or you are a columnist. The preference lay with the writer as was the case with Guha and Mehta.

And, the writers continued to do so, to make their choice, as Shiny Varghese invoked Nero while writing a comment piece on the Central Vista in The Indian Express, May 18, 2021, "Nothing in the project sees or hears the moments it set in. So, move aside Emperor Nero and Marie Antoinette, the people of India will have our own "Make in India" moment. When Indians ask for oxygen beds, lawns are being laid out. Until now, the people have stood still. It may be time to start walking." The piece was written when people were dying for lack of oxygen and due to Coronavirus. The hospitals had no space for patients and there was not enough space for cremation of people in the cremation grounds. The number of the dead at the cremation grounds and those provided by the government sources varied. The international media was carrying drone images of cremation grounds and the banks of the Ganges river that dotted with the floated and buried dead bodies.

It was therefore time for the writers to take their own call on their freedom to write or to bend as required. Senior journalists, who had enjoyed favours under the Congress regime and had been honoured with country's highest Padma awards, showed their back to it and joined the long list of unofficial spokespersons of the ruling party. They changed their loyalties and ingratiated themselves by clicking their selfies in an unabashed manner.

The Central Vista included a new parliament house reportedly devoid of the central hall where journalists mingled with politicians, looked for stories, and got political gossip. The space was reportedly not to the liking of the Modi government. It wanted to delete it. The Leader was averse to journalists. He instead preferred media organisation owners.

However, there were owners still who gave full editorial freedom or were themselves convinced to write on issues on merit rather than hold a grudge against any individual. But they were few and far between. They were ignored. The rest were on Modi's calling list. During the 2019-2021 Covid crisis, he preferred to speak to selected media owners rather than journalists.

Interestingly, even if he had called journalists for a chat, none of them would have asked an independent question. Ravish Kumar of NDTV was the lone voice against the government among the electronic media herd. However, his baiters too saw a reason behind his opposition. NDTV, it was said, was at loggerheads with the government because its promoters were facing charges on a number of financial irregularities.

The developments happened when the country was deep in the pandemic crisis and newspaper circulations were down by almost 70 per cent. Every paper was pushing content on online or on social media in a bid to retain their readership. Clippings were distributed by them to thousands of WhatsApp groups free of cost to retain the eye balls at least.

But ironically, in the post truth era, the clippings were circulated selectively on personal groups to serve the mischievous purpose of religious polarisation. The worst case was when the Republic TV anchor attacked Congress chief Sonia Gandhi over the lynching of Hindu seers in Palghar. The troll army was already out to term it communal violence instead of a case of mistaken identity.

Goswami crossed all limits of journalistic decency in one of his tweets which was retweeted by Congress leader Randeep Surjewala, "Aap ki party aur aapki party ke Rome se aaye hue Italy waali Sonia Gandhi chup nahin rahti. Aaj woh chup hain, man hi man main mujhe lagta hai woh khush hain... woh khush hain ki santon ko sadkon pe mara gaya jahan pe unki sarkar hai. Report bhejengi woh, woh Italy main report bheje gi … main bol raha hoon. Dekhiye jahan pe main eek sarkar bana li, wahan pe Hindu santon ko main marwa rahi hun. Aur wahan se wah-wahi milegi...wah beta..bohot acha kiya Sonia Gandhi Antonio Maino."

There were reports that Goswami was later assaulted by Congress workers on his way back home. He was booked in the Congress run Chhattisgarh for his comments. The scenario of a journalist being booked for its political commentary was not new but this was a never before kind of incident. Goswami was screaming from the rooftops and showering all kind of abuses on Congress and its leadership. If one was watching these channels, one would have got no inkling of the toll that the deadly Covid was taking in the country. The Maharashtra police, where Shiv Sena leader Udhav Thakre had formed the government with the support of the Congress, was accused of hounding Goswami.

On the other side, Saffron Sarkar went after professional journalists. A small town video journalist, who broke the

Namak Roti (mid-day meal) story, was booked by the UP police. A number of journalists also lost their jobs when they refused to fall in line while reporting on government decisions, or while writing, broadcasting on Prime Minister's office and its decisions.

Veteran anchor Punya Prasoon Vajpayee wrote he was asked by his channel, ABP News, to avoid mentioning Prime Minister Narendra Modi by name in his programme Master Stroke. When he refused to do so, he had to quit.

Needless to say that the incident happened when journalists and media houses had aligned themselves with political leaders while keeping the mask of journalism intact. The affiliation had turned so strong it became difficult to differentiate between journalists and workers of the BJP.

Social media was full of charges and counter charges on the issue and a number of anchors cautioned their colleagues that what had happened to Goswami could happen to them too. But the other group saw this as a deserving rap to Goswami who bullied one and all on his shows. No wonder, a majority of the journalists, who criticised the assault on Goswami, were the ones pursuing the state's line of thought.

But thwarting all accusations and abuses, the journalistic elite was undeterred and used their media platforms to perform loyalties to their political masters throwing ethics of journalism to the winds. While the country was battling the pandemic, a set of journalists were trying their best to investigate the religion of the pandemic.

And not only this, they were washing their dirty linen in public too. At an evening shouting show, June 25, 2020, an Aaj Tak anchor who got personal with a former anchor and Aam Aadmi Party politician, and currently a political analyst

Ashutosh over the state of journalism. Ashutosh said that the media was not doing its job in a fair and impartial manner.

He accused TV anchors, including the anchor on the show Dangal, of not asking questions to power, especially the Prime Minister. The anchor ineffectually tried to put up a brave face by countering the allegation saying Ashutosh himself had been asking all sorts of questions even to the Prime Minister while on this show. But he needed to hit him hard. He reminded Ashutosh he was the anchor who a politician had slapped publicly.

But Ashutosh was adamant and retorted saying that no anchor had the courage to ask questions to the Prime Minister and he quoted three former anchors of the ABP News who lost their jobs because they rubbed the government the wrong way.

Ashutosh's reply, infuriated the anchor. He charged Ashutosh with running a virtual Aam Aadmi Party election campaign while he was still an anchor with a news channel. The verbal skirmish turned ugly and personal. The IT cell got activated thereafter and released memes and short videos to embarrass Ashutosh.

This kind of situation was not confined to one channel. It was across the news media, with a couple of exceptions.

In the midst of the Coronavirus crisis, channels were busy doing a shabby investigation into the Sushant Singh Rajput suicide case when corona numbers were going up dramatically On a day when India recorded the highest number of cases—more than 77,000 – the entire TV media was relaying minute-by-minute details of the questioning of Sushant Rajput's girlfriend Rhea Chakarborty by the CBI.

And, it was also on this day that an India Today senior sub editor wrote to Prime Minister Narendra Modi about victimisation in his office by certain seniors who, he alleged, owed allegiance to the Left. His complaint failed to find place in any media due to obvious reasons. It floated on the social media where it was claimed that an investigation by a DSP level officer had been ordered after intervention from the PMO. The sub editor claimed a threat to life from his senior editors.

6

Stone-Cold Responses

In the middle of Covid-19 crisis, and at a time when the Central Government had initiated the country into yet another lockdown, Lockdown 4.0, Jai Prakash Nadda, president of the BJP, made a very important statement. He said criticism was a must for a healthy democracy while lashing out at the state governments run by Opposition parties. He alleged they were hampering relief work being undertaken by BJP workers. The states denied his charge.

His words, however, were music to the ears of many commentators and politicians who hoped Nadda's words of wisdom would reach his own political bosses, especially his predecessor, Amit Shah, who still carried enormous weight over party affairs.

In the heat of the moment to slam governments run by Opposition parties, Nadda seemed to have forgotten he headed a party charged with unprecedented intolerance towards its opponents. People opposed or in dissent with the government had been allegedly tormented, harassed, smeared on social media, and booked in various cases. In fact, the government had zero tolerance to any criticism, other than coming from their known opponents, branded as the anti-nationals — NDTV, The Wire etc.

The Covid-19 crisis exposed the government's ill-preparedness to manage it. There was severe mismanagement not only in handling the pandemic but also its fall out. Large-scale migration took place. It seemed to have failed to act as a welfare state and to manage provisioning and shelter for workers who had suddenly lost their jobs. Loss of work and pressure of the landlords for rentals, in utter disregard to the government's advisory to excuse people of rentals for the period of the lockdown, forced lakhs of workers to start walking to their home hundreds of kilometres away.

The government then failed to provide them safe passage and a number of migrants lost their lives during their miserable journey home. There were also tragic accidents. The most gruesome of them happened in Aurangabad in Maharashtra on May 8, 2020, where exhausted by their long walk, workers slept on the rail tracks presuming no trains were running due to the lockdown. Sixteen were run over by an empty goods trains in the wee hours of the morning.

The government eventually decided to run trains but a majority of migrants had no money to buy tickets. There were stories on how they had to sell off their belongings, household items, even their clothes, and electronic items to buy tickets. To rub it in further, the government initially opened online bookings only. The almost illiterate migrants had no access to online platforms and touts charged them exorbitant amounts for filling forms and getting their tickets done. After a brouhaha was raised over the sad situation, the government decided to hold camps where social distancing was thrown to the winds due to mismanagement.

Political panellists, on the other hand, made derisive comments and passed the buck to state governments, which, in turn, held the Centre responsible for the crisis. The deplorable spectacle of these migrants and their terrifying tales of starvation and death invited criticism of the government at the international level but little was done to provide substantive relief. Ironically, a whopping package of Rs 20 lakh crore was announced to meet the Corona crisis in the country by the Prime Minister yet it was not in sight on the ground. It was explained in an unnecessary elaboration by Finance Minister Nirmala Sitharaman on television for four consecutive days. Word power was however not backed by fund power in any which way.

Citizens though were moved by the unprecedented misery of migrant labourers on various national and state highways. The sight of men and women trudging barefoot, and in rags, with heavy baggage over their heads, small children trailing behind them haplessly, moved hearts nationally. Individuals rushed to help the exodus with food, shelter and medicine, but not the government. It avoided even the bare minimum response to this human tragedy.

It was, ironically, the same government that had proudly announced in Parliament that it was the first government to rescue Indians stranded overseas free of cost. Special airplanes were flown to bring back Indians from Covid-19 epicentre of Wuhan in China. Later, planes were sent to Japan, Italy and other countries. The government spent crores of rupees to mount the rescue operation, Minister of State for External Affairs V Muraleedharan informed the Lok Sabha. "Air India has raised a bill of Rs 5.98 crore for operating two special flights to China."

Migrant labourers, the poorest of the poor, however, were made to pay extra for returning home. The government did not bother to extend a kind gesture to them.

In a video chat with the Chief Ministers, Prime Minister Narendra Modi said, "We stressed that people should stay where they are. But it is human nature to want to go home so we had to modify or change our decisions."

Brinda Karat, a Rajya Sabha MP and Politburo Member of the CPI (M) frowned on the PM Cares Fund and asked whose care the fund was taking if not of the poor people.

She wrote in an article, "The Prime Minister has set up a PM Cares Find. Hundreds of crores of rupees have been donated to this fund. We can only make guesses since the actual amount is not in the public domain. Why is this money not being used to bring the workers home? Whose care is the PM interested in if not that of India's labour force, or rather, India's life force who are the creators of wealth?"

The Supreme Court of India, where a petition was filed urging it to direct the Centre to provide food and shelter to the migrants on their way home after they have left their place of work due to the sudden financial crisis, dismissed the petition. The court said, "How can anyone stop this when they sleep on railway tracks? How do you stop migrants who want to keep walking?"

The court also observed that it was not possible for it to monitor the situation and it was up to the state governments to manage the situation. The court order received stifled response for the fear of contempt but The Hindustan Times carried an edit that was frank to call it mismanagement and failure of political executive. It also wanted the court to be more sensitive on the issue.

It said, "Irrespective of the merits of the petition in question, the observations fit into a larger pattern of the court's attitude towards the issue. It has accepted the claims of the executive too willingly; it could have done more to order relief and protective measures; and it should have ensured strict court monitoring of the entire process of identification of migrant workers, provision of food and shelter either where they are based or during their travel, and their transport. To their credit, in the backdrop of workers having to wait for as long as 19 hours to board trains, the Gujarat High Court observed that there was lack of coordination among government departments on the issue and asked the government to be more sensitive to the plight of the most 'downtrodden, underprivileged and weaker sections of society,' and instil confidence in them. The Karnataka High Court has also done well in observing that workers can't be deprived the opportunity of travelling home because of their inability to pay fares. India's poorest need help. The government has to do its bit. But the courts can help, with more sensitivity and direction."

Leading legal luminary Fali S Nariman noted with concern the attitude of the Supreme Court over the problem of migrants walking home. "Earlier three orders separately passed by different benches of the highest court had declined to give any direction to the majoritarian government at the Centre to make transport available to migrant workers; it also failed to suo motu implead the concerned states so as to enable the apex court to issue directions to the state governments to ensure humanitarian relief and bring an end to the degrading spectacle of starving migrant workers walking hundreds of miles to their homes." Nariman gave plenty of arguments in support of his observation but the government had become immune to any such suggestions.

Interestingly, Solicitor General Tushar Mehta arguing on behalf of the central government called the petitioners `prophets of doom` in the apex court and questioned the contribution of senior lawyer and Congress leader Kapil Sibal while urging him not to `make it a political platform.' Sibal's answer to the question was, "Four crores. That's my contribution."

Mehta was deeply critical of those who asked the court to intervene, said a report in The Indian Express, May 29, 2020. Mehta said, "A large number of steps were taken by the government and the Supreme Court was fully satisfied about it earlier. But we have something called prophets of doom who only spread negativity, negativity and negativity. All these people writing on social media, giving interviews cannot even acknowledge what is being done... They are not showing any courtesy to the nation. State governments and ministers are working overnight. None of these people acknowledge (them)."

While trying to make his point, and after raising the national flag when he grudged about lack of courtesy to the nation, Mehta also invoked South African photographer Kevin Carter who clicked the Pulitzer winning photograph of the vulture and the little girl, but later committed suicide.

The Indian Express was most eloquent in a hard-hitting edit on Mehta's sweeping statement in the court. "Yet, on a day when the country's highest court finally, if belatedly, questioned the Centre and the states on the plight of stranded migrant workers, it takes a particularly blind and blatant partisanship, apart from a moral obtuseness, to question, instead, the commitment and credentials of those who are pointing to the unfolding tragedy and calling for urgent redress and accountability."

This was true that the courts agreed to take stock of the plight of the migrants after their misery and hardship spread across the roads of the country evoking strong reaction from every quarter, including a number of ruling party members who preferred to remain quiet on public platforms for fear of action from their political bosses. The Express edit went ahead and warranted Supreme Court action on Mehta's statement. "Of course, there will always be someone in the Bar or in the PIL cottage industry who gives out integrity certificates to the judiciary and quickly takes them back, depending on which way a particular verdict goes. But it's a bit rich for Mehta, as counsel for the government, to lecture the bench — and the world — on what judicial independence should mean. There is a question, too, for the Supreme Court. The SG's outburst draws attention to the SC's silence. It would be unfortunate, indeed, if the SG's unwise and mean-spirited exuberance is allowed to be seen to, in some way, or in any way, be endorsed by the highest court."

The Prime Minister, on the day the article appeared, was to conduct an aerial visit of the devastation caused in West Bengal, which was next to go to the assembly polls, by cyclone Amphan. People were critical of this aerial visit on social media but the government was hardly bothered.

Sensitivity in the time of the Sarkar was not the only virtue discarded by its leaders. They survived on the daily dose of steroids, which included ridicule, cynicism, sarcasm and insults, which they hurled at the Opposition leaders.

After the Supreme Court observation, which was widely considered to be insensitive, it was the turn of party's Hindutva icon and Chief Minister of Uttar Pradesh Yogi Aditya Nath to ground buses provided by the Congress to transport migrant workers. It found faults with the list of registration numbers given by the Congress general secretary Priyanka Gandhi.

The state claimed the list had numbers of three wheelers, bikes and transport vehicles, besides buses. Wrong numbers on the list could have been dealt with later and genuine buses could have been made available immediately. But Yogi was more interested in a political fracas than a desire to help the helpless.

Though the BJP missed no opportunity to promise Ram Rajya in the country, it failed to provide safe and comfortable passage to migrant workers who are instrumental in raising swanky multi storied buildings in the national capital. The top BJP leadership was busy writing articles in the newspapers hailing their leader when an unprecedented human tragedy was unfolding before their eyes.

An incredibly cold-hearted response was thus witnessed in the country that was known for its compassion and humanitarian values. The BJP's idea of Ram Rajya, it was obvious, ended with the guarantee of a colossal statue of Lord Rama at his birthplace in Ayodhya.

7

Holier Than Thou

The Modi machine drummed up a shrill holier-than-thou campaign from the time of the 2014 elections. The masses were initially taken in by the propaganda; but as realization dawned on them that they had been taken for a ride, it was too late. The government had won the second term in 2019.

In 2014, Modi built up a narrative around how the Congress had destroyed institutions in the country. It had only worked towards serving its vested interests. It was corrupt to the core, Modi had alleged. He was particularly uncharitable about the Gandhi family, especially Sonia Gandhi and her children. He blamed the '70 years of Congress' for his government's failures.

Whether it was the ill-thought decision to demonetise the currency or the falling GDP and other economic indices, including rising unemployment and poverty, Modi passed on its failures to the past Congress governments. They had not primed up the country enough to absorb the impact of his policies for a New India.

Modi was miserably failing on all fronts but instead of taking corrective action he wished to succeed in pinning the blame of his failings on the Congress and the former Prime Minister Manmohan Singh and of course Jawahar Lal Nehru.

It was his best plank to swim against the rising tide of public criticism.

The ruling party also failed to coordinate within itself. Statements on the Chinese intrusion in Galvan valley by Prime Minister Narendra Modi and Defence Minister Rajnath Singh differed from each other. While the Defence minister said the Chinese army had trespassed into Indian territory, the Prime Minister claimed otherwise. But instead of sorting out the contradictory claims and speaking the truth, the party attacked the Gandhi family for accepting a donation from China for the Rajiv Gandhi Foundation. Needless to say that it was actually a bait for the channels and by the evening it was the only issue discussed on prime time, Chinese donation to Gandhi Trust.

BJP president Jagat Prakash Nadda hurled a set of ten questions at the Congress on the funding of the Rajiv Gandhi Foundation, which, he alleged, had accepted Rs 20 lakh in donations from China years ago. Interestingly, Nadda's press conference was held at a time when the country was witnessing an unprecedented hike in petrol and diesel prices. On June 27, 2020, when Nadda held his press conference, fuel prices had been hiked for the 21st consecutive day. But he said nothing about it. Instead, he went hammer and tong at the Congress.

Baba Ram Dev, who had once been an ardent critic of the Congress government for failing to curb petrol prices, and had promised on Modi's behalf that BJP would reduce petrol prices once it came to power, unabashedly justified the hike. Without batting an eyelid he said, "Keemten kam honi chahiyen par akhir Modiji ko desh bhi chalana hai, revenue to fuel se hi aata hai (Prices should be contained but Modi has to run the government too; after all, revenue comes from fuel sales.)."

Beaming anchors ran the footage live and within minutes were throwing questions to Congress spokespersons on the financial situation in the country.

Former Finance Minister P Chidambaram, who was on bail under the Modi regime for his alleged financial bunglings, though asked: "If RGF returned Rs 20 lakh, will China recall its troops?" Several Congress leaders then raised the issue of funding of the BJP through electoral bonds, and to the RSS from various foreign sources.

Bonds become a major issue and shattered the BJP facade of honesty and transparency just ahead of the 2024 Lok Sabha elections after the apex court held the bond unconstitutional and said that voters had the right to know who gave whom and how much donation.

There was hardly any doubt that Modi's policy to appease China by his frequent visits and by hosting Xi Jinping time and again in India had failed. Opposition parties listed his visits to China and said he should explain the reasons which necessitated him to visit China four times as Chief Minister and five times as Prime Minister.

Renowned international political columnist Brahama Chellany wrote in The Japan Times, June 8, 2020, "Indian Prime Minister Narendra Modi is 'not in a good mood,' US president Donald Trump recently declared, and offered to mediate in India's resurgent border conflict with China. After years of bending backward to appease China, Modi has received yet another Chinese encroachment on Indian territory. Will this be enough to persuade him to change his approach?"

The New York Times carried a piece, headlined, `China's military provokes its neighbours but the message is for United States.' But the Indian media asked no questions nor did it analyse the ground situation factually. Especially the visual media.

Prime Minister Modi, at the beginning of the controversy, said China had not intruded in Indian territory. The statement came after India lost 20 army men in hand- to- hand combat with the Chinese army. The Chinese quickly latched on to the PM's statement. Chinese media said it showed that India intruded into Chinese areas. The Chinese government too was quick to stake claim to the Galwan valley.

The NYT piece by Stevan Lee Myers on June 26, 2020, clearly mentioned that China was creating a situation of military clash with its neighbourhood and their claims that their military actions were in defensive were nothing but a farce. It said, "China claims all of its recent operations are defensive, but each increases the risk of a military clash, whether intended or not. That appears to be what happened on the night of June 15, when Chinese and Indian soldiers fought along their disputed border in the Himalayas. It was the bloodiest clash on that frontier since 1967. According to Chinese analysts, Indian news reports and American intelligence reports, it also caused an undisclosed number of Chinese deaths, the country's first in combat since its war with Vietnam in 1979."

Pratap Bhanu Mehta wrote in The Indian Express, June 16, 2020, ``The Republic of India is facing a leadership crisis.... the crises are challenging. But they are made more intractable by the fact that India has a leadership deficit at the top. India's political tragedy is that even the depth of the crises cannot be acknowledged. The government fully understands that to even acknowledge any elements of the crisis would be to puncture its legitimising myth, that India is in the hands of a powerful leadership that was going to be the sole vehicle for its manifest destiny. Whereas the blunt truth is that there has almost never been a time in India's recent history when it was so bereft of leadership."

But the news channels had a different narrative. They ran with the divisionary tactics of the government ignoring pressing security, economic and social issues. The big question however was how the selected narrative found its way to all the channels simultaneously? Was there some sort of standing instructions as the evening debate on RGF donation was taken up within minutes of the Nadda press conference on various channels? Had the channels been briefed about the press interaction hours prior to the actual event and told to ready their pitch for the evening? The ruling party spokespersons were fully armed too while mounting their attack on the Congress.

An anchor told this author, ``It is not easy to pinpoint the source of such invisible command, as most of the time it cascades to the anchors from the top. To be specific, it would flow to the number two from top, and then from two to three and so on. Also, there are some prominent TV personalities who have had past associations with the ruling party's frontal organisations or have the same viewpoint as that of the government."

Modi did not address the nation on Chinese intrusion though he did a Man ki Baat radio address. He invoked former Congress Prime Minister Narsimha Rao to temporarily bail out the country from criticism on the China front. Though Narsimha Rao found a glowing mention, the word China was conspicuously missing from the talk. More importantly, the Prime Minister praised Congressman Rao while castigating the Congress for its 70 years of misrule. He deliberately overlooked the fact the Rao was Congress PM in five of these 70 years, or that BJP's Atal Behari Vajpayee was PM for six years too during the said period.

8

The Fifth Pillar

Social media emerged not only as a strong dissenting voice but also established itself as the Fifth Pillar when the Fourth Pillar was crumbling.

At the height of the Indo-China crisis over Galvan valley, Prime Minister Narendra Modi landed in Ladakh. The print media carried the Press Information Bureau press note on the visit in verbatim. The Prime Minister was in Ladakh to laud and inspire security forces and to put China on notice. This was the common line taken by all the channels and newspapers. They used the videos and pictures provided by the PIB. Reporters on ground filed stories as they were told by officials, including Modi's visit to the Leh hospital where he met soldiers who had been injured in the Galwan clash.

Social media, however, went into a frenzy. It pointed out that Modi was nowhere near the LoC despite the official claims. He visited Leh which was 255 kilometers away from the Galvan valley. It quickly rubbished reports about the modern hospital that Modi had visited. It pointed out, through archival photo galleries, that the so-called hospital ward was in fact a conference room converted into a makeshift hospital room for PM's photo op.

Social media activists pointed out that the purported photo of the hospital ward had an overhead projector that is used for conferences and the room had no dustbins, no provisions of drip and oxygen cylinders. Moreover, the `patients` were sitting in a meditative position. The Prime Minister also had a sound system to address a small number of 'patients' in a small room!

At the soldiers' rally in Leh, the PM spoke of everything except the Chinese intrusion. He did not utter the word 'China' even once though he had visited soldiers injured by Chinese intruders a short while ago. Social media referred to the amiss repeatedly but the news channels had their own script. 'Ab karara jawab milega dragon ko,' one channel headlined its special programme, another was quick with its short video snippet that showed Xi Jinpin biting the dust and dragon running with its tail between the legs!

Netizens were eager to know why the 'barking brigade' that often activated itself on Pakistan by naming and shaming the neighbouring country was silent on China? Spokespersons of other parties too wanted to know the reason and compulsion in not naming China.

Intriguingly, it was Defence Minister Rajnath Singh who was scheduled to visit Leh after the clash with Chinese soldiers in Galwan. But his visit was cancelled at the last moment. It was superseded by the PM's visit. The man in command then proceeded to turn a blind eye towards the killer of 20 soldiers of the Indian Army.

The period of Corona crisis was very important for the social media. Prime Minister Narendra Modi had always underlined the importance of the social media. But the heavens started to fall when, during the crisis. Modi's `Mann ki Baat` on Youtube failed to get enough likes. The dislikes outnumbered likes in thousands.

In this episode of the monthly radio talk, Modi asked people to become vocal for local toys. He exhorted them to manufacture toys to capture this promising market. He also praised desi breed of dogs. The IT managers of the government were astonished by the severely hostile response. Youtube was asked by the government to disable likes/dislikes/comments for Mann ki Baat.

The government also shot off a letter to Facebook founder Mark Zuckerberg complaining that the firm's India team was acting against those supportive of the right-of-centre ideas. The then Union Minister Ravi Shankar Prasad wrote to the FB CEO that Facebook's India team was dominated by people who belonged to a particular political belief.

Interestingly, this was one area where the saffron party had the same view on FB as its arch rival, the Congress. The party had also accused FB of political bias with Rahul Gandhi alleging that Facebook and BJP were in nexus to manipulate opinion.

Prasad, on his part wrote, ''I have been informed that in the run up to 2019 general elections, there was a concerted effort by Facebook India management to not just delete pages or substantially reduce reach but also offer no records or right of appeal to affected people who are supportive of the right-of-the-centre ideology. I'm also aware that dozens of emails written to Facebook management received no response."

Ironically, the Modi government alleged Facebook bias after six years in power, and after it started losing popularity on social media.

9

Forced Narrative

"Would you believe a reporter or the Prime Minister of the country?" BJP spokesperson Sambit Patra shouted at the Congress spokesperson after she challenged the government claim that not even an inch of land was captured by China on the Ladakh border.

The Chinese aggression was debated after the Indian army successfully thwarted an attempt by the Peoples Liberation Army (PLA) to escalate the situation at Pangong Tso and change the status quo on the South Bank of the lake.

Anchors, who had been over busy covering actor Sushant Singh Rajput death case, suddenly changed tack and trained their vocal chords on China and how Prime Minister Narendra Modi had given it a karara jawab — befitting reply. Ironically, the Prime Minister had only obliquely referred to China, and stopped short of taking its name in his speeches on the border crisis.

Patra's self-righteous comment was a reaction to The Hindu report of September 21, 2020, which said China now actually controlled an additional 1,000 sq. km territory in Ladakh. His remark was typical of the party's tirade against journalists. It also underlined that the words of the Prime

Minister were not up for any scrutiny. They had to be taken as Gospel Truth.

The Hindu story was based on Intelligence sources of the government. It said, "About 1,000 square kilometres of area in Ladakh along the Line of Actual Control (LAC) is now under Chinese control, intelligence inputs provided to the Centre suggest." It also claimed China was amassing troops and fortifying its presence along the LAC since April-May, 2021. Twenty Indian soldiers had also been killed in hand-to-hand combat in Galwan valley when they pushed the PLA troops back from Indian territory.

But his was not the only issues. Freedom of expression was another. The Supreme Court had taken up the issue of senior lawyer Prashant Bhushan tweeting about Chief Justice of India posing on an expensive Harley Davidson motorcycle. Bhushan, in his tweet, criticised the CJI and some of his predecessors for their public conduct. The apex court took up the tweet as contempt of court.

After a long debate, the court directed Bhushan to tender his apology to escape contempt proceedings. But, by then Bhushan was a social media hero; his case found adequate support in print media. Bhushan refused to apologise. But there was not a line on it in TV news.

The court then held Bhushan in contempt, and imposed a fine of Rs 1 on him. The court said that failure to deposit fine would result in three months imprisonment and debarment of Bhushan's licence to practice for three years.

The pronouncement invited stinging edits in newspapers the next morning (September 1, 2020). The Hindustan Times titled its edit, `The SC sets a wrong precedent`, and said, "The SC bench led by Justice Arun Mishra has unequivocally said that Mr Bhushan made, 'reckless allegations', capable of 'shaking the very edifice of the judicial administration.' It has limited the boundaries of free speech, saying criticism of judiciary must be 'measured, strictly rational, sober and proceed from the highest motives without being coloured by partisan spirit or pressure tactics or intimidatory attitude."

The HT edit further said, "A victory for those who believed in free speech would have been a review of the order itself. The case represented an opportunity to set right the contempt jurisdiction. Unfortunately, the court has ended up setting a wrong precedent."

The Hindu also felt the Supreme Court, by sentencing Bhushan, diminished its stature and thus exposed its intolerant side. The edit concluded, "The proceeding was fated to shine a light on the Court's conduct rather than on the actions of the contemnor. In the ultimate analysis, it is not a verdict that purges Mr Bhushan of any contempt. Rather, it comes across as an unfair, but inevitable punishment for his refusal to apologise or express regret for his opinions on the conduct of judiciary in the recent years."

Print media apart, television channels, except NDTV, did not report even one sentence of the contempt case.

During the Corona crisis, the GDP of the country for the April-June quarter of 2020 slumped to a record low of minus 23.9 per cent. Finance Minister Nirmala Sitharaman, instead of offering a roadmap to revamp the economy, called Corona virus an Act of God.

Interestingly, in 1952, when a thick fog engulfed London, Prime Minister Winston Churchill labelled it an Act of God. He nearly lost his job over the crisis though he soon realised that he was mandated by the people to act on the crisis rather than pass the buck to God. In India, however, no channel attempted an evening discussion on the Covid-19 issue. It rather busied itself in deflecting the audience from the crisis.

Newspaper circulation was limited during the Corona crisis due to logistical reasons. Electronic media could have filled the breach and highlighted major issues facing the nation — the threat to free speech, falling GDP, unemployment, price rise, etc. But its priority was the drug connection of actress Rhea Chakaborty and her brother. Rhea was a friend of Sushant Singh Rajput. TV channels went berserk over the supposed 'story.' They became reporter, witness, investigator and judge. Barring an exception, non-stop coverage of the 'story' was unleashed in the race to gain TRPs at any cost. The tragic death of a film star was encashed abashedly for institutional gain. The broadcasting regulatory authority preferred to look away rather than rein in the coverage.

TV channels swung like a yo-yo between the stories on drug abuse in film industry and the fake narrative of muscular nationalism. Sample this ABP headline (September 1, 2020), "Cheen ka kaal bane Doval." Similar headlines streamed on the screens of nearly all other channels. A little later, they swung to the other end shouting maniacally, ``Mujhe drugs do, mujhe drugs do."

Ironically, majority of the anchors were seen to be pushing forced narratives which actually aimed at fending off the government from the possible attack on a policy failure or the rhetoric of the ruling party leader, by the opposition. Critics were calling this period as the bhakti kaal of politics. Factually, this breed of journalists had been prospering in every government but in this it was seen with an unabashed hubris. Anchors seemed to be enjoying their little descriptor, the Godi media.

And in the mid of all this, a leak that claimed that the government had prepared a detailed `toolkit` for media management sent a number of journalists, ministers, and the government in tizzy. The sheer number of those present in such meetings where it was proposed to colour code the journalists was discussed, was enough to leak it, as you know black sheep, it may be anywhere, everywhere. The leak was an embarrassment not only for the journalists but for the organisations too whose senior editors and bureau members were present besides the former heads of media organisations.

The story was broken by The Hindustan Times though later it was revealed in news report that in first such meeting held on June 23, 2020 at the residence of Union Minister Kiren Rijiju, the Executive Editor of the Hindustan Times Shishir Gupta was also present. The story was later followed up elaborately by The Caravan, The Wire and The Newsclick in the first week of March 2021. The Indian Express too carried a story headlined: "GoM's good news plan: Colour-code journalists, `neutralise` the negative. Stories carried on other media platforms mentioned that an Indian Express journalist was also present in one such meeting. The Express wrote, " One of those who attended the June 26 meeting and is named in the report was Ravish Tiwari, Political Editor and National Bureau Chief, The Indian Express. "The meeting was called at Minister Rijiju's residence as a background briefing with External Affairs Minister Jaishankar on the stand-off at the Line of Actual Control," said Tiwari. "No one mentioned anything about a GoM. When I reached, we were told that the External Affairs Minister was caught up and couldn't make it." The story also stated "There was some talk about lack of information-sharing about the LAC stand-off," said Tiwari. "The Minister, based on his past experience as MoS, Home, discussed the LAC but that was off the record. I am surprised how an off-the-record briefing on LAC has been presented as part of a GoM meeting." Surprise, Surprise!

The Wire story said, "In a series of meetings held last year when the pandemic was at its peak, the Union government set a mandate for its ministers and secretaries to identify, track and control its critics in the media and social media, promote journalists, websites and commentators helping the official narrative, and engage "positive influencers" on social media, retired journalists, and "former army generals" to "turn the narratives" in its favour."

What else would be required to prove that the government always intended to push a forced narrative through its own journalists especially in the electronic media. The party and organisation ideologues present in the meeting wanted not only to use the media resources available to them but also to involve NDA allies to make the narrative looked genuine and credible. In a way, it was admitting that the people have stopped trusting the official narrative. It was also an admission that the channels that were now being identified their own were losing their credibility and hence the narrative needed independent voices to support it.

The government was under severe attack or its cack-handed response to the COVID 19 spread. The RSS ideologue S. Gurumurthy's words reportedly said at the meeting were enough to prove the point. His words also proved that the ruling elite was worried over the fact that their supporting channels were turning to be the pariahs, "Planned communication is good for normal times but to create Pokhran effect, let Shri Nitish Kumar or Shri Naveen Patnaik say something about it. This is being done by Republic, but Republic is seen as a pariah. Therefore, we need a Pokhran to turn the narrative."

This meeting discussed the execrable suggestion of colour code the journalists on the basis of their allegiance and how to treat them on the basis of their classification. The Hindustan

Times story hardly drew any attention but after the news portals took it in a big way certain media houses too took up the story but with their own version. It was The Wire that carried extensive parts of the story along with names of all the journalists who participated in the meeting.

According to The Wire report, " Shekhar Iyer reportedly said that since the relationship between the editor and the government has been traditionally "adversarial", the government could cultivate reporters who could explain a fact-based build up leading to major decisions by the government. This, according to him, could solve the problem of adversarial reporting.

How to counter digital media's adversarial reporting formed the crux of former Prasar Bharati chairman A. Surya Prakash's suggestions too, according to the report. "The party spokespersons or bureaucrats should be trained to handle media to create counter to the digital media narrative. We need separate platform particularly to engage with the literate class. Therefore, social media/digital platforms should be taken on priority," he reportedly said."

However, it is not that the meeting was all about castigating the journalism and wailing over the adversarial reporting by the adversarial journos. A sane proposal was made at the meeting, another matter, that nobody paid any heed to it and the menace on the editorial pages of the mainstream newspapers continued to be contaminated by the Sarkari press notes written by ghost writers under the bylines of the ministers.

The Wire report said, "While recommending that ministers should stop writing op-eds in newspapers as they are hardly read with seriousness, the former press secretary to the President, Ashok Malik, reportedly offered an alternative.

"Have spokespersons for clusters of Ministries to provide background information to spin the stories. For example, outward looking Ministries like MEA, Commerce etc; social sector Ministries like Health and Family Welfare, Education etc; Economic clusters: Political narratives like CAA, NRC, environment, and green energy. These clusters should have spokespersons who can be anyone, viz., Ministers, Advisors, Academicians, Bureaucrats and they should be working 24×7," he said.

The meeting that was reportedly attended by a number of senior former editors besides senior editors and bureau members working with the leading and mainstream newspapers. No wonder, whoever was approached though admitted to have participated in the meeting but denied the reported purpose of the meeting.

10

Tracking Traitors

Dissent not sedition, can't try citizens for anti-govt views: SC American Watchdog on democracy rates India as `partly free` I-T searches premises of Tapsee, Kashyap

The Times of India carried these three headlines on March 4, 2021. Most newspapers carried extensive reports on the three instances, and also wrote editorials on the sedition law and its irrelevance to present-day democracy. The edits reminded the government that the British introduced the sedition law to repress Indian freedom fighters. They were also informed that even the British had got rid of this archaic provision. The reminders were ignored. The government was bent on tracking 'traitors.' It needed no advice on who the 'traitors' were.

From news point of view, all the three stories were the most important stories of the day that warranted national attention. But TV news channels picked up only one — IT searches on the premises of film producer-director Anurag Kashyap and actress Tapsee Pannu. The two had been steadfast in their critique of Modi government policies.

The Sarkar was particularly unhappy with Tapsee's support on social media to the ongoing farmers' agitation against the farm bills brought in by the government. Farmers from various parts of the country, particularly from Punjab, Haryana and UP, were on a continuous dharna on the Delhi border against the new laws.

The government was finding it difficult to tackle the situation on the ground as support for the farmers had breached national borders. Celebrity endorsement for the farmers' cause became global after American pop singer Rihanna and Meera Harris, niece of US Vice President Kamala Harris, tweeted in their favour.

Given the background, news TV went into a frenzy during their evening debates speculating on the IT searches and claimed the Kashyab and Pannu were sitting on a pile of black money. The evening 'debate' was part of the smear campaign against the two Bollywood celebrities as they had dared to question government policies and actions.

The channels were unconcerned about other two prominent stories of the day. None of them debated, or even reported, the Supreme Court's observation on sedition law. They also did not mention the case of Disha Ravi, a young environmental activist, who had been promptly arrested by the Delhi Police for editing a toolkit which allegedly contained Internet resources for spreading the word on the farmers' agitation.

The court took the Delhi Police to task for booking Disha on the basis of scanty and sketchy evidence. LiveLaw reported, "Considering the scanty and sketchy evidence available on record, I do not find any palpable reasons to breach the general rule of bail against a 22- year old young lady, with absolutely blemish free criminal antecedents and having firm roots in the society, and send her to jail."

The court also observed that nothing indicated that the toolkit was forwarding any secessionist agenda. It said,

"The perusal of the said 'Toolkit' reveals that any call for any kind of violence is conspicuously absent. In my considered opinion, citizens are conscience-keepers of government in any democratic nation. They cannot be put behind the bars simply because they choose to disagree with the State policies. The offence of sedition cannot be invoked to minister to the wounded vanity of the governments."

In another case, former Chief Minister of Jammu and Kashmir Farooq Abdullah had been booked for his statement on the scrapping of Article 370 of the Indian Constitution by the government.

Dismissing a petition that alleged that Abdullah's statements post scrapping of Article 370 were anti-national and seditious, the Supreme Court said, "The expression of a view which is a dissent from a decision taken by the Central Government itself can't be said to be seditious."The story was not carried by channels because it ran counter to the official narrative which classed every dissenter as an anti-national person.

Similarly, when Washington-based global democracy watchdog Freedom House downgraded India in its annual ratings; Sweden's V-Dem called India an electoral autocracy, Prime Minister Narendra Modi was quick to point out the 'foreign hand' behind conspiracies to defame his regime.

The country was by then in electoral cacophony in the states of West Bengal, Assam, Tamil Nadu, Kerala and Puducherry. The BJP leadership was bending its sinews in West Bengal particularly to oust the two-term Chief Minister Mamata Banerjee and establish itself firmly in the state for the first time.

Aiding and supporting the BJP's bid for power in the

five states were hyper active TV channels. The visual media were out baying for blood of those 'foreigners' who had raised their concern about the farmers' agitation. The channels accused Meera Harris of Hindu Phobia. She dryly tweeted her response, "Dude, I'm Hindu. Stop using religion as a cover for fascism."

And, in the case of Rihanna, Monica Gill wrote on her twitter handle, "Modi spokesperson Sambit Patra is throwing fits on Republic TV, saying, 'WHY DIDNT RIHANNA TWEET IN 1984?'All bhakts are highly impressed and clapping. Rihanna was born in 1988, and Twitter started in 2006. Rihanna has at least managed to expose the IQ level of Indian bhakts."

The response was not reported by news channels which played and replayed the government stand that international figures had no locus standi in India's internal matters. Bollywood stars such as Akshay Kumar and Kangana Ranaut were also activated to counter remarks made by internationally known persons. The damage control had assumed great importance because of the forthcoming assembly elections in five states, including West Bengal and Assam.

Election time was also a marketing opportunity for news channels. They set up shops (debate venues) in important constituencies in the states where the anchor interacted with the local population with the official agenda firmly in place. Huge advertising support was made available for such TV shows. The plan however backfired to a certain extent when the attendees started protesting against the narrative pushed by the star anchors.

Public outcry against unadulterated bias was witnessed throughout the farmers' agitation. Agitators refused to speak to TV reporters and loudly castigated them for toeing the government line. At Singhu border, where farmers created a record of sorts by their unique protest, anchors were shouted down, people also raised slogans such as 'godi media wapas jao' against private news channels.

Reporters freely admitted that they were being forced by their bosses to 'twist' stories on the agitation in order to defame the farmers. A reporter of a leading news channel was so conscious-striken by the lies he was forced to tell on screen every day that he climbed the farmers' stage and publicly resigned his position. But then majority anchors belonged to the category where they ran their evening debates to castigate the farmers. Sample this, during the second wave of the Coronavirus, farmers staged their protest observing `black day` against Central Government's adamant attitude towards the agitation.

The Aaj Tak's leading anchor Anjana Om Kashyap ran her evening show with the opening, "Yes you have the right to protest. But in the time of the deadly virus when people are dying. Won't it pose a serious danger to the other people?" And she was not the only one. Others too were following her line. Unfortunately, she was in for a shock as farmer leader Rakesh Tikait took the anchor duo Kashyap and Chitra Tripathi to the task with his spontaneous and rustic response laced in acid. Here are the excerpts:

AOA: It is true that democracy gives the right to protest. But one infected person can infect a number of others. Rakesh Tikait ji do you know this? Tell me what is your agenda? What is going in your mind? Because the circumstances are scaring the people.

RT: And what about press? Would they work as the spokespersons of the BJP? They won't be bothered about the protest for three months. What are you talking about? All are working for BJP as their spokespersons. This country is seeing you as well. Now you would invoke Corona. Blame it on farmers......Delhi should hear this loud and clear. These press people are spewing rubbish. We are seeing them for the last three months. They are working like BJP spokespersons and people of the country are seeing them.

CT: Is the present situation allows to continue this agitation? Why this agitation be not deferred for the welfare and security of the common man?

RT: Would the government give a guarantee Corona would vanish from the country if agitation was withdrawn? Corona is a disease, its cure is in the hospital.

It was the first that the new and aspirational India which had that emphatically chanted 'Modi Modi' in 2014 and 2019, changed it to 'Godi, Godi' to express its displeasure with the media.

Digital media was a saving grace to a large extent though. In fact, social media became a solid weapon to hit at the government.

Interestingly, before things got to such a pass, India's young brigade was full of Modi love. They liked his macho image and bold utterances such as 'ghar me ghus ke marenge.' It gave them an adrenaline rush. Nothing else, it seemed, mattered to them. Arbitrary decision making, unemployment, job losses, demonetisation, a savage lockdown, migration that almost killed the economy and disturbed the lives of the common man, etc. had not dented Modi's image in any substantial manner.

But things changed following the farmers` agitation. New, young felt betrayed. It was disillusioned by the government and the leader. Thus far, no more. The incensed youth turned against the BJP, and in western UP, Punjab and Haryana party leaders were not allowed to enter villages. They were pushed away from their functions, they were compelled to divert their routes, choppers were not allowed to land at the venues of their political rallies.

Things became embarrassing for the Haryana Government when BJP leaders were chased out of their public meetings. Chief Minister M.L. Khattar and his deputy Dushyant Chautala were not allowed to land at the venue of their rallies. No wonder that this was carried till the 2024 Lok Sabha elections when BJP leaders including Khattar, who was dethroned days before elections were not allowed in Haryana villages.

However, during the agitation youngsters were out in streets raising slogans against the Prime Minister, writing songs criticising his handling of the farmers' agitation. These songs put the social media on fire. People even started playing the songs at their marriages. Memes on the agitation flooded the social media.

No leading TV media ventured to capture these protests for obvious reasons; it didn't suit their agenda, and there was protest against them, too. Prominent anchors, who tried to approach the venue of agitation for 'coverage' and had previously labelled the protestors as khalistanis, were forced back with farmers playing 'Hoya ki je bik gya India da media, BBC de utte jhote chhaye hoye ne (What if the Indian media is sold we have captured the space on BBC.)' at full volume. The song routine started when young environment activist Greta Thunberg tweeted in favour of the farmers' agitation.

Interestingly, while the anchors did a number of shows on how the farmers were putting themselves and others at grave risk by violating the Corona protocol, they evaded asking the questions to mask-less BJP leaders holding huge public rallies.

They sometimes questioned BJP leaders, but with an apprehension of retribution. The questions were also usually supplied by the ruling party whenever it wanted to confuse an issue raised by the Opposition.

A prominent anchor questioned a top BJP leader, "Opposition parties are alleging that your son is allegedly involved in a scam. Is there some truth in it or has it been provoked by their imminent defeat in the elections?" The leader responded to only the second half of the question in which he dwelt at length on the frustration of the Opposition parties at not being able to get peoples' support in the polls.

Another anchor boarded the electoral rath of a top BJP leader and was more elated over the crowd than the leader himself. She described the scene thus, "Yeh thathe marta samandar. Aisa lagta hai aap chunav pehle hi jeet chuke hain ya koi gunjayash hai? (This sea of human faces! It seems you have already won this election or is there anything still amiss?)." The leader smiled benignly at her. The anchor had reported her views as 'news,' once again.

However, at a time when the ruling party was trying to track the traitors in every sphere including media of course from among the virodhi media, analysts were trying to identify the elected autocrats. And this search was not confined to one country but was an international hunt. In his study on elected autocrats, as similar tendencies were witnessed in various countries especially in the United States where former president Donald Trump came in the eye of the storm for his negligent and careless response to the spread of Coronavirus. Besides Trump, president of Brazil Jair Bolsonaro too came under attack for his reckless attitude to the deadly virus and because of what the virus took a number of lives in Brazil.

Patrick Heller, a professor of Sociology and International Affairs, that appeared as main edit piece in The Hindu, June 1, 2021, Heller listed three common traits of the elected autocrats. And he brought Prime Minister Narendra Modi too under the ambit of an elected autocrat. Heller identified three elected autocrats in former US President Donald Trump, President of Brazil Jair Bolsonaro and Indian Prime Minister Narendra Modi on the basis of his study.

"First, they came to power as classic right wing populists who branded themselves as incarnations of the people and peddled their personal virtues of strength and fortitude as substitutes for deliberation and policy making. Rulers with Messianic faith have little patience for experts and science. All three have surrounded themselves with yes-men and ruled from the gut, peddling triumphalism, (all three prematurely declared the pandemic vanquished), quack remedis (injecting disinfectants, the waters of Ganga) and sheer macho bombast."

(Remember exit of Raghuram Rajan, Arvind Panagarhia, Arvind Subramaniam and claim that India excelled in surgery in ancient times and Lord Ganesha was the first example of surgical intervention. And yes-men, of course, uncountable)

"Second, autocrats feed on polarisation. All three have championed a virtuous nationalism - rooted alternatively in evangelism in Brazil and the US, or Hindutva in India— animated and weaponised by the demonisation of the other. Ethnicised nationalism works by demoting the "other"— Muslims, Blacks, immigrants, gays, secularists and all those who subscribe to ideals of civic nationalism - to the status of the undeserving and the morally efficient.....Mr Modi has a long record of debasing India's 200 million, and when re-elected in 2019, doubled down on his party's platform of making India a Hindutva project, first by turning Kashmir

(India's only Muslim majority state) into a militarised colony of Central Government and then pursuing laws that are perceived by Muslims according them second class citizenship status."

Needless to say that elections in India had never been so polarised. The political parties were successful in vertically dividing the voters on the lines of their religion, caste and creed. Religious slogans galore in every election from the municipal committees to the Parliament.

Third, once in power, the autocrats quickly personalised, centralised and insulated their power. All three have attacked the Constitution (literally in Mr Trump's case) demanded fealty from independent, overridden the authority of expert institutions, tampered with data, assaulted the independence of the media and elevated loyalty to the leader as the highest principle of service.

No wonder, that with a slight push on the memory chip of mind we would find examples on every count in the country. Every institution, the executive, the media, the judiciary, the election commission of India etc suffered the accusation of being under duress and acting on behalf of the Sarkar.

11

TRP Tilt

"Frankly speaking, I cannot stand it. This has never been part of our public discourse,`` the Chief Justice of India commented while hearing an appeal filed by the Maharashtra Government challenging a stay order on an investigation against television presenter Arnab Goswami, The Hindustan Times reported on October 27, 2020.

The Chief Justice was referring to the high decibel prime time debates on channels where mutual decency had been blown to smithereens. Interestingly, 'Frankly speaking' was the title of Arnab Goswami's evening debate. The channel's lawyer, Harish Salve, agreed with the court, "Responsible journalism is covering sensitive issues without sensationalising. It is better to remain old fashioned."

But this was hardly the case with Republic TV which aired debates with brutal disregard to a person's individual freedoms. It regularly carried sustained campaigns, which were nothing but witch hunts. A few among the affected parties knocked at the door of courts for relief.

Arnab Goswami pioneered the trend of hurling invectives at not only his panellists but also on public personalities. He was particularly vitriolic towards Opposition parties while loudly pushing the narrative of the BJP. Perhaps at the behest of the powerful government caucus, other channels began to mimic Republic TV. Their motivated rants surrounded viewers from all sides.

Amidst the sound and fury generated by channels over false narratives; and shrill, uncivilised hectoring from anchors, the TRP scam hit the fan. Mumbai police claimed that certain channels indulged in rigging of the Tele Rating Points (TRP) metre in order to earn more revenue on the basis of fudged data. Mumbai police named Republic TV as one of the accused. It triggered a never- before kind of confrontation between the channel and the police. Goswami attacked the police alleging it was a conspiracy hatched by the non-BJP government in Maharashtra to attack the freedom of media.

The Mumbai police crime branch named Republic TV, News Nation and Maha Movie as accused in the alleged manipulation of TRP data. Initially, no names or designations of the accused were mentioned in the FIR but as the confrontation raged, Mumbai Police registered a fresh FIR against Republic TV executive editor, anchor, two reporters and other editorial staff for relaying 'false and baseless news' that incited disaffection among police personnel against their chief Param Bir Singh.

It also charged the channel with tarnishing and maligning the image of the police in public. The case was registered under section 3 (1) of The Police (Incitement and Disaffection) Act 1922 and sections 500 of Defamation Act and 34 of the Indian Penal Code.

Goswami was livid at the dare, and challenged the police and the government. He alleged bias and pointed a finger at Mumbai Police Commissioner Param Bir Singh for targeting the channel. He also flayed the Shiv Sena-led coalition government of Maharashtra.

As the prime time debate on Republic TV focused on the TRP scam, the police raided the residence of Goswami in the wee hours of November 4, 2020 as a follow up on a an old abetment to suicide case that had been closed by the police earlier. Goswami alleged he was manhandled during the process of arrest. He got no relief from the lower courts and the High Court on his bail application. His lawyers then approached the Supreme Court, which granted him bail.

Justice DY Chandrachud observed orally while granting bail to Goswami on November 11, 2020, "People are now put in jail for a tweet... We are travelling through the path of destruction of liberty. You may not like his ideology. Left to myself, I will not watch his channel. But citizens are sent to jail, High Courts don't grant bail. We have to send a strong message."

Justice Chandrachud also asked senior advocate Kapil Sibal, who appeared for Maharashtra, "There has to be an active incitement to make a case of abetment to suicide. A person has not paid – does this amount to an act of abetment to suicide? Can a person be sent to custodial interrogation, whoever it is..."

The Hindu, raised certain questions on the apex court order. It echoed the feeling of a number of journalists, civil liberties activists and intellectuals when it wrote: "The Supreme Court has struck a blow to personal liberty. Granting interim bail to television anchor Arnab Goswami through an order that one wished would also be passed in the case of many others incarcerated without sufficient cause, and with the same priority, consideration and speed. ``

The timing of the petition for interim bail was also questioned in the edit piece. "In Mr Goswami's case, the Session Court was due to hear his bail petition the same time the matter was before the High Court. Therefore, it is somewhat strange that the petition was posted immediately for hearing and that interim bail, pending a reasoned judgment, should be granted on the same day. Further, Justice DY Chandrachud's observation, `If we don't interfere in this case today, we will walk on a path of destruction,' seems out of place in a case that clearly does not relate to Mr Goswami's journalistic work. Surely, a scrutiny of why such consideration or sympathy has not been shown for others held mainly for their political beliefs or journalistic work is warranted. It is not idle whataboutery to point out that it was only recently that the apex court turned down a petition for bail on medical grounds to lawyer-activist Sudha Bhardwaj and sent it to the High Court with a gratuitous observation, 'You have a good case on merits. Why don't you file a regular bail application?'"

It also said, "The court's recent record of evading and postponing hearing on many matters concerning fundamental rights and constitutional questions that affect the rights of large sections of society is a veritable story of judicial abdication. It is somewhat galling to note that its gladiatorial zeal for personal liberty is demonstrated in so selective a manner."

G R Gopinath, in his article in The Hindu, November 12, 2020, too raised questions over Republic TV crying foul over the arrest of its editor and held a mirror to the channel supporters, and to the channel itself, "The channel, until Wednesday, was crying itself hoarse that its anchor's arrest was a threat to the free speech and strikes at the very foundations of democracy by muzzling the freedom of press. This is also ironic considering that the channel is notorious for shouting down those who hold an opinion at variance to the anchor. The channel that never raised its voice in defence of many of their journalist colleagues when they were arrested, assaulted, some jailed on improbable charges of sedition, and a few even killed, began taking refuge in amnesia."

At the time when The Hindu raised these questions, every anchor on the channel was screaming that the arrest had shaken the democratic foundations of the country. BJP netas, from Amit Shah to Rakesh Sinha, were worried over the way the arrest muzzled free speech and how it posed serious danger to the democratic structure of the country. Ironically, this narrative was created by the ruling party for a channel that was notorious for shouting down dissenting voices!

As was expected, when Goswami was released on bail, he raised slogans `Bharat Mata ki jai' and 'Vande Matram.' His release was not covered by any channels, except NDTV.

However, bail to him did not close the chapter for the commentariat and legal eagles. A former judge of the Delhi High Court Rekha Sharma, The Indian Express, February 6, 2021, raised the issue questioning the alacrity with which the apex court allowed bail to the TV anchor. "While Arnab Goswami got interim bail from the SC with alacrity in a case of abetment to suicide on the principle 'bail, not jail, is the rule', many bail petitions are not taken up for hearing. Take Kappan's case. The bench headed by the CJI reportedly said the court wanted to discourage Article 32 writ petitions for such matters, and Kappan thus was told to go back to the concerned High Court. Incidentally, B R Ambedkar described Article 32 as the 'heart and soul of the Constitution.'"

Ever since two new channels — Republic TV and TV9 Bharatvarsh — were launched, mainstream channels, which had dominated top positions on TRP charts, especially Aaj Tak, were uneasy. The new channels had a loud pro establishment tone and were brazenly taking sides in debates. Since other channels too were toeing the same line, the new entrants crowded their space. TV9 Bharatvarsha was launched by Prime Minister Narendra Modi. Though TV9 was a bit squeamish about its affiliation, Republic TV wore it like a badge of honor.

If there were any doubts regarding its deep nexus with the ruling dispensation, it was exposed in mid-January 2021 when the Mumbai Police submitted the alleged Whatsapp chat between Arnab Goswami and Broadcast audience Research Council (BARC) CEO Partho Dasgupta. Screenshots of the purported chat between the two popped up on every small and big screen.

Goswami said boastfully, "All ministers are with us." The chats revealed that the TV anchor was privy to confidential and top secret information too. He apparently had advance information on ministers to be inducted into the Union Cabinet. In a May 2017 chat, Goswami told Dasgupta about developments in the Ministry of Information and Broadcasting and disclosed the name of Venkaiah Naidu as the next Vice President. The same day BJP Parliamentary Board picked Naidu as Vice President.

And if this was not enough, The Indian Express on January 25, 2021 carried a story headlined, 'Arnab Goswami paid me $12,000 and Rs 40 lakh to fix ratings: Partho Dasgupta.' This money, the story said, was paid for two separate holidays over three years in return for manipulating ratings in favour of the news channel.

The story also quoted Dasgupta's statement recorded with the Crime Intelligence Unit in which he said, ``I have known Arnab Goswqami since 2004. We used to work together in Times Now. I joined BARC as CEO in 2013. Arnab Goswami launched Republic in 2017. Even before launching Republic TV, he would talk to me about plans for the launch and indirectly hint at helping him to get good ratings to his channel. Goswami knew very well that I know how the TRP system works. He also alluded to helping me out in future." Dasgupta's lawyer denied the allegations in the same story, and, later, Goswami sued the Indian Express.

However, soon after these chats showed up on social media, the ruling party understood the need to distance itself from the alleged statements in which the anchor flaunted his close proximity to the ministers. The party however continued to harp on the veracity of the chats and claimed Partho Dasgupta's statement was recorded under duress.

As per The Indian Express story, Republic TV was not the only news channel which tilted TRPs in its favour as the BARC forensic report named several news channels, including Republic, Times Now and Aaj Tak. There was indeed an unholy nexus.

The real problem with country's visual media industry was that it never introduced reforms ever since its conception more than two decades ago. The previous Congress government had been magnanimous in granting licences to channels. The number of channels reached a whopping figure of 912 by the end of 2020. Nearly 400 channels of these are focused on providing news and current affairs content and it is needless to say that a majority of these are free to air or charged a nominal fee.

As such, the industry heavily depended on advertising revenue. Its programming therefore frequently swung between news content and commercial new content. The situation reached such proportions that it became difficult to ascertain the difference between advertisement and professional news content.

Programmes like `Adbhut, Avashvisniya and Akalpniya` or astrological predictions or dramatised crime-based episodes such as Sansani, Crime Patrol, Crime Reporter, etc. or the ridiculous coverage of violence in Panchkula at the time of the arrest of Baba Gurmeet Ram Rahim ruled the roast.

The programming was aimed at grabbing the lion's share from an estimated Rs 40,000 crore revenue pie of TV media. Like the Indian democracy, where politicians did everything moral/immoral to get a single vote, the media industry too did not shy from rigging the system to its advantage.

It was easy to beat the system with the muscle of influence and money. It was therefore not surprising when a labourer's home was found to have an LED and a muted English news channel installed in it. When questioned, the person, as reported by the police, said nonchalantly, "The money I get to keep it switched on is good."

Not that the central government was unaware of this rigging but it kept quiet as it suited its interest. The Telecom Regulatory Authority recommended change in the system thrice but it evoked no response from the government. The Centre's stand came up during a hearing on Sudarshan TV's 10-part series that alleged Muslims were infiltrating the civil services.

The Centre that had made a fervent attempt to regulate social media said, "Considering the serious impact and the potential, it is desirable that if the SC decides to undertake the exercise, it should first be undertaken with regard to digital media as there already exists sufficient framework and judicial pronouncements with regard to electronic media and print media."

The social media was more vocal on government's flaws than the channels which heavily depended on the government not only for their revenue but for their existence as well.

Social media, on the other hand, did not depend on advertisement revenue from a particular government. Its revenue came from private enterprise or funding. Also, there was no official or unofficial content regulation, especially on the individually subscribed social media platforms such as WhatsApp, Instagram, Facebook, etc.

12

Bad is Good

Social media, especially over the last decade, developed its own norms. Here you are known by the numbers, larger the number of your followers, greater is your popularity. The Sarkar had been judging its ministers by the number of their Twitter followers or the hits they took on their eulogising videos, they were praised over their strength in numbers and snubbed for their lack of numbers. The politics reduced between the clicks and hits. And the same was the case with the anchors, they were after the number of hits and gave two hoots to the quality of a debate.

One very significant development took place during this time that majority of the leaders became immune to any shame or embarrassment over their online castigation or ridicule, as even the trolls and abuse too increased their number. This was applicable for all including the journalists especially those working for the online media or were running their own portals and of course the anchors. Their partisan and bias provoked panellists to insult and humiliate them on the live shows. Hooligans started disturbing their live public debates in the poll bound areas and panellists attacked them for their alleged biased and slanted journalism on their live shows.

The television journalism took a new low with every passing day but nobody was bothered as long as it perked up their TRP. There was no attempt to conceal their allegiance to the parties and leaders. People identified the anchors as pro Congress or anti BJP, same on the lines of one particular channel's daily rant of Godi media and virodhi media. You would constantly listen and be bored with this specific line, "godi media will not show you this, will not show you that, we are showing you and then it would display a number of stories from English newspapers.

However, point is that such videos which would actually be cause of shame and embarrassment were put on youtube and on online media to grab more eyeballs in a shameless way. No amount of social media snub could prevent the anchors to desist from taking an open and unabashed posture in favour of the Sarkar. But for anchors it was the moment of their glory on social media.

Anjana Om Kashyap of Aaj Tak was trolled on social media for her pro Sarkar stand and it deeply affected her and things came to a pass that while starting her programme `Halla Bol` she inadvertently said, "Hello Halla Bol. Today, I am with you, Anjana Om Modi." No wonder, her trolls swelled.

Aaj Tak ran a programme titled, "Nusrat pooja ko razi, kya karega quazi"

The debate was focused on Nusrat Jahan's dance in the Durga Puja Pandal in Kolkata.

Host: Anjana Om Kashyap

AOA: If Nusrat applied vermillion and danced in worship to Durga then what was the point of worry? Why such gesture is spread as hatred?

In another debate one of the guests Shoeb Jamai frowned over the sanctity of a question and asked the same anchor whether she was asking question on behalf of the ruling party. Here is how it happened:

Shoeb Jamai: Anjana ji I know you are a prominent journalist. Entire country listens to you. I have a small query that whether this question is from your side or the BJP's?

Programme host was visibly upset over the sudden and unexpected question. She snapped, "This question is from whom? This is obviously from my side. Do I need to give in writing? Your appetite is spoiled to an extent that every question seem to you from BJP. This is Anjana Om Kashyap's question and that is that whether a woman can't dance?"

SJ: You should not feel bad.

AOA: Why not? Nobody can raise a question on me. Why did you say that I was asking question on behalf of a party? Why did you ask? You lie also. How dare you ask such a question?

The guest is heard saying `BJP BJP` in the background.

AOA: Don't be stupid with me in future.

SJ: Anjana ji I said so because this is a conspiracy.

AOA: Don't be mean. You are called here to answer the questions. I shall ask you such questions a hundred time. In case a woman.....How dare you ask this. You are asking me that I was asking a question on whose behalf. Are you in the BJP office? Don't you know which studio have you come? Nobody raises questions on male members. Don't you dare.

SJ: I am a citizen of the country.

AOA: You are a citizen. Is this licence to mud-slinging? Every right has a responsibility. Read the Constitution. You are so engrossed in religious books that you don't know the Constitution.

This prime time anchor of Aaj Tak had been in controversy and blamed for working for the BJP. After the assembly elections, Rajasthan Congress government was seen in danger. Gaurav Bhatia of BJP and Pawan Khera of the Congress in debate at a show hosted by Anjana Om Kashyap. This was a high octane heated debate in which Khera accused the anchor of working for the BJP.

AOA: Pawan ji what fear is bothering Ashok Gehlot? He is saying that BJP was repeating Madhya Pradesh here (Rajasthan)?

PK: Anjana ji earlier if somebody planned to topple a government then the media would condemn such effort. What is your topic? Your topic is to consolidate the BJP. Nothing else. If somebody is grabbing country's land (a reference to China occupying Indian territory), there would be no concern to save country's territory but to save the BJP. You have made mockery of the journalism. You don't have courage to ask questions to the powers that be. If you really have some strength then pose your questions to the power. Show some mettle.

AOA: I have enough strength. You can't even guess how much courage. But I know your courage.

PK: It's easy to ask the opposition. You won't dare ask questions from those in power. Don't teach me journalism. Don't teach me politics. Also, don't compel me to speak. I know the reality of the media.

AOA: your mouth is always open. Don't threaten me. Answer my question. This debate would be good if I said yes to all your observations.

This Aaj Tak anchor perhaps had record of controversial videos. She was, however, on an embarrassing pitch at Sahitya Aaj Tak with Shayar and Bollywood script writer Javed Akhtar.

AOA: From Bollywood to media, to common man, to a tea shop. Everybody is divided on nationalism. Thoughts, words, everything.

JA: What should we do with the tea shop? Media, this all. By all of a sudden you have gone to a chai ki dukan (tea shop)?

The jibe was clearly on the Prime Minister Narendra Modi who proudly declared that he had been selling tea at the railway station during his initial years.

AOA: This virus seemed to have reached Bollywood too. There are quite a few nationalist director, producer, nationalist actors and a few are said be in love with Pakistan.

JA: You consider Bollywood a zoo where you find certain amazing animals. What is Bollywood? There are every type of people who hold different views. What do you want that everybody should think on similar lines. Then this country is not for you. You should better go to Saudi Arabia.

AOS: Can I dare...?

JA: And what were you doing so far?

AOA: You read first poem, Sazish (conspiracy). Hope this not a conspiracy to turn the history over.

JA: Which one?

AOA: To change the names of cities. To create a controversy in the name of Tipu Sultan.

JA: No, nothing. These things are superficial. These happen. You too get the TRP. Had you not thumped that much table on that. By the way how many programmes you did on that?

AOA: You have done a bit of injustice with media.

JA: Oh my my. You will criticise the world from morning to evening but won't tolerate a word about you.

Javed Akhtar was getting thunderous response on his smart answers which was quite an opposite as it happened to be the home ground of anchor. Visibly on backfoot, Anjana conceded, "You, sir, seemed to have felt the pulse of the audience.

JA: You do this effort from morning to evening but if you fail to get it then what should I do?

Another round of applause for the veteran poet who cornered the host with ruthless agility and smartness to steal the show. The organisers were sulking at the end of their wits.

Importantly, channel managements never get alerted over such negative publicity as for them it was money minting stupidity. On the back of the prime time anchors who became the centre of social media ridicule, humiliation, embarrassment, sulk and memes, even their own colleagues would laugh out loud but on their face they would thumbs up for them. Anchors feigned ignorance over such negative connotations over their short snippets and charged their online perpetrators as jealous and nuisance makers.

A nationwide lockdown was imposed upon the country that was yet hearing the reverberating proud slogans of Namaste Trump. Till a day before, the country was bravely facing the Coronavirus and suddenly the lockdown. And then the sudden and shocking showed its fallout on the highways, as thousands of labourers headed for their homes on foot. employees were asked to go on leave. A number of employees lost their jobs. Contractual labour was asked not to come. And in the mid of this chaos, Sarkar announced to relay Ramayan and Mahabharat in an obvious bid to divert people from the other vital issues, they were suddenly faced with.

A former television actress and then Union Minister Samriti Irani posted a video, singing a song, and exhorted people to play Antakshari in their homes. The ploy came under attack on social media but then suddenly two prime time anchors Shweta Singh and Anjana Om Kashyap of Aaj Tak started playing Antakshari on the screen. Here goes the highlights.

SS: We have shown you some amazing videos and now is the turn of Antakshari. My colleague Anjana Om Kashyap too is live now. Anjana what we had been playing during our childhood, you must remember it. So I am starting it:

Samay bitane ke liye karna hai kuchh kaam

Shuru karo Antakshari le kar Aaj Tak ka naam

So its M

AOA: So I have to sing a song starting with M. OK.

Mere Saamne wali khirki me, ek chaand ka tukra rehta hai....

I think it's better to keep away for sometime. So Shweta, you stay in your window and your neighbour in own window.

SS: For that purpose I maintained social distance from you.

AOA: Yes social distancing is essential. You, everybody should stay home safely. And my song too is saying the same thing.

The channels seemed to be totally oblivious to what was happening in the media in and out of the country. Or it was their brief to look away from all this and kept them immersed in the shallow waters of low grade debates to push the state's agenda. While in job they never expressed it but once out of it they came open. This was what happened when ABP News shunted out its two top anchors and one producer allegedly after they refused to push the programmes on dotted lines. One of the anchors charged the owners with interference. It was difficult but he took a stand and shared his concern about this state of affairs in the channels. Other channels too were not exceptions but not that someone came out to divulge the reasons of ouster and instead they quietly made their way out.

A former Zee TV journalist Vishwa Deepak revealed in a lengthy open letter to its management before quitting his job and raised the issue of the existential crisis for the journalists.

Read this in his words reported at a website, "So much so that I am assailed by a deep doubt whether we are journalists anymore. It seems as though we are the mouthpiece of the government.... An agenda behind every news, an attempt to deify the Modi government as great in every news show, an attempt in every debate to shoot down Modi opponents – no lesser word than attack is acceptable to us. What is all this?"

Vishwa Deepak raised the question, answer to which was not very difficult to find and ostensibly he too has realised the same before taking the extreme step that would have marred his career.

Thanks to their visible bias and blatant partiality towards the ruling party, majority anchors lost their credibility and face in the public. But they were not worried about it, as this was not what they were vying for, they aimed at making their masters happy and were not bothered about any public humiliation or even insult as long as they succeeded in their mission.

Emboldened by the deeply slanted and tilted style of anchoring, panellists were openly called names to the anchors who had no option but to bear insult. A live debate on News18 between late Congress spokesperson Rajiv Tyagi and anchor Amish Devgan raised quite a storm and was cause of worry for the journalism. Both became hyper and accused each other with screaming and shouting. See for yourself:

RT: The debate has already gone for 15 minutes. "Please give me uninterrupted one and half a minute.....(disturbance after six seconds), should I complete? you are an intelligent anchor. I hope you would be impartial too.

AD: (Shoutingly) You are not on a tea shop of a street or a mohalla.

RT: Amish Devgan, if you are not to listen to us then why do you call us?

AD: I called you because I want to listen to you.

RT: Stop speaking like a middleman, like a pimp.

AD: Stop threatening.

RT: (Repeating his accusation) Stop speaking like a middleman or a pimp. Behave like a journalist.

A cacophony broke over his comments. He was asked to take back his words to which Rajiv Tyagi replied.

RT: No my friend, I call you a middleman. I call you a pimp. What else, you are a broker. Amish Devgan took a break and after the break he again asked Rajiv Tyagi whether he would apologise or regret for his behaviour to which Tyagi replied,

"Absolutely not. I am rock-solid on what I said.

At loss of face, Devgan time and again asked him to regret or apologise and Rajiv Tyagi said, "I have used two words for you and if you would compel me then I would repeat them again."

This became a routine as panellists while shooting their verbal shafts on the anchors considered them their target because they placed them alongside the ruling party. Insults hurled with impunity on the live TV debates but no anchor or the editor or the owner seemed worried about this because this was what they actually wanted. So much so that such debate obviously rocked the TRP charts so they repeated their telecast besides putting them on their websites, youtube channels or on their social media handles. And if a channel or the anchor failed to do so then the panellist would tweet it from his or her own handle or through their Facebook page.

However, this did not confine between the anchor and the guest. But there had been instances when panellists collided between themselves. In a few cases it came to blows between them, mutually abusive language was commonplace and in a few cases matter reached at the level of the police station.

One such instance can be seen in the below mentioned verbal duel between Congress spokesperson Ragini Naik and BJP spokesman Gaurav Bhatia. The debate was on the inadequate availability of vaccines in the country.

RN: Now please let me speak. This Badtameez (stupid) person should not speak in between again.

GB: Badtameez aurat hato yahan se. (You stupid woman go away)

Continuous commotion between the two. Anchor keeps quiet, perhaps enjoying.

RN: Sadak chhap ghatiya aadmi pahle mujhe....

Her voice dies in the din

GB: You are stupid, your leaders stupid. Your leader is pappu, pappu....

RN: Muh me daant tumhare nazar nahi aate, totle aadmi, champu, chup ho jao.

(Your teeth are not seen in your mouth. You stutter, better you be quiet)

Alka Lamba who left Aam Aadmi Party to join the Congress was livid on Aaj Tak over the alleged agenda journalism of the channels. And this is what happened:

Alka Lamba to Anjana Om Kashyap: You have your own agendas. And that's why Congress stopped coming to your channel. I came in my own individual capacity as a woman.

AOA: Don't make it dramatic.

AL: Shame on you Aaj Tak. Shame on you Anjana.

She then boycotted the live debate.

Deepak Chaurasia's case was unique. One still had his picture in an astronaut's gear during the live telecast of the launch of the Chandrayaan II, India's orbiter-lander-Rover mission in October 2019. As usual, all leaders were out doling out interviews on the eve of the Lok Sabha elections in 2019, before the second coming of the NDA government under Prime Minister Narendra Modi. Needless to say that journalists too were handpicked to give interviews. Chaurasia interviewed the Prime Minister on his channel News Nation. To expose the preset interview, alt.news founder Prateek Sinha wrote on his twitter handle along with the screen shot of a paper which contained the question and the answer too. He said that PM Modi read a poem in this interview and when he asked for the file then it was visible that on the upper part of the paper, the question was written. The question was, "Towards the end I want to ask the poet Narendra Modi whether he had written something in the past five years?" It seemed that the Prime Minister was given the questions in advance.

For the news channels things went that awry that they were barred from the protest sites for their pro-establishment behaviour. Social media was abuzz with a Jawahar Lal Nehru University clip in which students were shoving the leading news channels while raising slogans, "Godi media wapas jao." Zee News Editor Sudhir Chaudhary and senior TV journalist Deepak Chaurasia were not allowed to enter the Shaheen Bagh protest site. Farmers at Singhu border disallowed majority leading channels from covering their protest and openly charged them with bias and partiality. In short videos made at the site of protest, majority media channels barring the NDTV were mocked and ridiculed. However, this ridicule and insult was not confined with the opposite parties but it cascaded in their live programmes and with their own panellists too. Anchors were routinely chastened by the experts and opposition members for their lack of courage to ask questions from the powers that be.

TV Journalist turned politician turned expert Ashutosh was at his wit's end when he collided head on with Aaj Tak's anchor Late Rohit Sardana. The debate turned alarmingly personalised It seemed that evening debates were nothing but a friendly mud-slinging match. Here it goes:

RS: You are in this programme. I won't ask how many other programmes you go or you don't go. But as many times as you sit on this channel, had anyone stopped you from asking any question? Did anyone asked you why did you ask this or that about Modi or Amit Shah? Did anyone stopped you from asking anything about Narendra Modi? Had ever Narenrda Modi's aide came to ask you, Ashutosh bhai why did you speak this or that? Were you pressurised? Or any notice served upon you under the IT Act for carrying something on your website?

Ashutosh: Now you have asked a very sensitive question. I would appreciate you if you would ask about Chinese intrusion in Indian territory while holding the Prime Minister responsible? Rohit Sardana, I challenge you to ask two/three questions.

RS: You throw challenges like a street fighter. Ashutosh ji what were you doing when you were sitting at my place? (Ashutosh was a former anchor)

Ashutosh: Why did Punya Prasoon Vajpayee lost his job? Why did Abhisar Sharma lost his job?

RS: You may say that you lost your job because you asked a government a certain question. Though everybody knows that you quit your job because you wanted to contest election. (Ashutosh had joined the AAP and lost Lok Sabha election after quitting his job) Not only this you were accused of propagating a certain party as an editor on your channel for two years. Why are you using such person's shoulder? You are projecting them as martyrs? Debate is not about them or how did they lost their job.

Ashutosh: What Indira Gandhi did after imposing emergency, you are doing the same but without imposing emergency or it would not have happened that a journalist would write something and be charged with sedition.

RS: You are talking about sedition. You are that man whom a leader slapped. You mean at that time there was freedom but now we lack that kind of freedom.

Ashutosh: Kanshi Ram (It was Kanshi Ram who slapped Ashutosh) later apologised to me.

RS: Despite being a journalist, you joined the electoral fray. You say it on TV that you don't have freedom. You write on your website that you don't have freedom. You make a video and upload it on Facebook saying you don't have freedom. I don't understand what type of freedom do you want? You want to scream it from above a water tank?

Later, Ashutosh asked on his twitter handle that there were how many dalit reporters?

Rohit Sardana was quick to respond, "While recruiting as an Editor, how many times did you ask the applicants to show their caste certificates?

13

Fakery

A year after the lockdown was introduced in the country, the Boom did a fact check on how the Indian media was picking up false and misleading stories during the period. A fact-check report of the website reproduced by The Wire named almost all Hindi news channels for abetting the fakery. The list included Aaj Tak, ABP News, Republic, Zee, India TV, News 18, and TV9 Bharatvarsh.

Earlier, The Wire carried a list of top ten fake stories in 2017. The list included a story relayed on the Zee TV that claimed that Nostradamus had predicted about the coming of Prime Minister Narendra Modi. It claimed Nostradamus had said, "The supreme leader of India will be born in the state of Gujarat. His father will sell tea in a shop. His first name will be Narendus." The wire reported, "Even as everyone was having a good laugh about Narendus, Vajpayum, Advanum and Murlum Joshum, Zee News found it to be an entirely believable tale, worthy of sharing with its viewers."

The list also included a story broadcast on Aaj Tak about the issuance of a fatwa in Saudi Arabia which entitled men to eat their wives if they were hungry. And, of course. a Republic TV story claimed that Jama Masjid electricity was cut off because of non- payment of a Rs 4-crore bill.

The case of Sudhir Chaudhary of Zee TV was the most curious. In this classic fake story, Chaudhary told his viewers about the nano GPS chip installed in the newly printed Rs 2000 currency notes. He explained it in detail: "The government has used a state of the art nano technology to stop the flow of black money into the economic system. This is something new. Every Rs 2000 note will have a nano GPS chip. We will also tell you how this technique would work. This chip won't require any power source to work. It works like a signal reflector. Whenever a satellite sends a signal to know the location of this chip, it reflects the signal. This way the government will get the exact location of the currency along with the serial number. Hence, this currency can now be traced even if you conceal it within the proverbial seven locks. Even if the currency is buried deep — 120 meters — the signal will reflect it. So, the Rs 2000 note will now bring you to the rule of law despite your best efforts to conceal it."

The bedlam of a fish market took multiple avatars on the small screen. On the one side, a panellist swears before the camera in a live debate, and, on the other side, an anchor intrudes in the Intensive Care Unit of a hospital with the camera pointed like a missile. They were trying to relay cheap filmy sort of clips to the viewers in order to catch attention from their 'exclusive' footage. However, usually on such occasions they ended up looking embarrassed. But then it was the time of shame- proof journalism.

14

Ninnies' Dum Dum

The May of 2021 brought to the fore, in the most glaring and tragic way, Modi Sarkar's inept handling of the Covid-19 crisis. There was utter chaos in hospitals as the daily count of patients and deaths rose dramatically. There was not enough oxygen, or medicines for patients. People, in urban and rural areas, died like flies. Telling images of burning ghats choked with dead bodies and the Ganga full of bloated bodies showed how badly the government had botched up its Covid policy. International media was full of stories of unprecedented governmental neglect. The Prime Minister himself was under severe attack, not only from the Opposition, but even from his supporters. The boastful bravado was smashed to smithereens by one fell swoop of Covid crisis.

But the government was still adamant. It did not swing into action to help its stricken population. It, instead, brought in a 'Toolkit' that was being allegedly used by the Congress to 'defame' the government on its failure. The BJP's loud spokesperson Sambit Patra and a few other senior leaders and ministers alleged that this `Toolkit` was prepared by the Congress to malign and defame the Prime Minister. The Congress denied the allegation. Its head of social media Rohan

Gupta filed a complaint with the police alleging the `Toolkit` was a fake.

Interestingly, Twitter had already marked `Toolkit` tweets by the BJP leaders, including that of Sambit Patra, as 'manipulated media.' Twitter's action infuriated the BJP, and, on May 24, 2021, a team of Delhi Police's special cell under the Home Ministry visited the offices of Twitter in Delhi and Gurgaon to investigate the `Toolkit` controversy.

TV anchors fanned the BJP narrative on the issue and castigated the Congress for stooping to a low level of politics. The BJP traced one page to a Congress worker and the anchors were more interested in discussing the particular page than taking up the 'Toolkit' controversy in its entirety.

Social media companies such as Facebook and Facebook-owned WhatsApp were already at loggerheads with the Central Government over the new guidelines that warranted the companies to regulate their content and appoint grievance compliance and liaison officers for compliance of the new IT rules. The new digital ethics rules made it mandatory for the companies to take down objectionable content within 36 hours. The companies were also made responsible for submitting the compliance report to the government. The move would have landed major players in a soup as they had immunity so far against third party content posted on their apps.

WhatsApp challenged the new rule 4 (2) of the Information Technology (Intermediary Guidelines and Digital Media Ethics Code) Rules, 2021,and said it would violate its end- to-end encryption and was an invasion on the privacy of the users.

Privacy in India has been a contentious issue in the past but on August 24, 2017, the Supreme Court of India put at rest all debate when it declared it a Fundamental Right in a landmark judgment pronounced by a nine- member bench. The court unanimously declared null and void all previous judgments that stated that right to privacy was not a Fundamental Right. The WhatsApp called the new rules an infringement on the Fundamental Rights of its users. The company petitioned that the new rules would violate the privacy of users as it required social media companies to divulge the identity of the originator of the objectionable information on demand from the authorities.

The government was adamant on its stand and issued a statement that the WhatsApp petition was nothing but an act of defiance and an attempt to stall the Act. Union Information and Technology Minister Ravi Shankar Prasad launched a counter offensive against the company saying that the government was committed to the right of privacy but at the same time it also had the responsibility of maintaining law and order and preserving national security. It also stated the right to privacy was not absolute. The government expressed astonishment over WhatsApp's resistance to the new rules while some other countries already had restrictions along the same lines.

A day after, on May 27, Twitter expressed concern over the security of its employees following police visit to its offices in Delhi and Gurgaon. "We are concerned for our employees and freedom of speech in India," said Twitter, adding there was "potential threat to the freedom of expression" of its users in India. It also called the police visit on its offices 'intimidation.'

The Union Government slammed Twitter for its attempt to dictate terms to world's largest democracy. It also said that Twitter's defiance was actually aimed at arranging protection from any criminal liability. It also claimed that Twitter policies were opaque and policy matters are the prerogative of the sovereign. The Delhi police called the WhatsApp statement on its visit to the Twitter offices as misleading. "The company is not truthful and is only trying to obstruct the police inquiry in to a Congress complaint against the `Toolkit` conspiracy aimed at smearing the image of the Prime Minister."

Interestingly, when WhatsApp revised its agreement with the users to allow them to share their data with its parent company Facebook, a number of people started deleting the app. It later made this agreement optional and assured that no data would be shared without their consent. The company also assured users it was committed to end- to- end encryption of messages.

The Modi government that had been the darling of national and international media had its first bad taste of international press when a number of overseas newspapers took it to task for its all fingers and thumbs response to the second wave of Covid- 19 spread. The entire foreign ministry was deployed to counter the situation.

KP Nayar, a strategic analyst who has been foreign correspondent in various countries for over three decades, wrote in The Tribune, May 10, 2021, "In the old days, when the media and India's government officials were not adversaries, the Acting Australian High Commissioner would have invited the newspaper's Editor-in-Chief, or more likely, the journalist who wrote the searing indictment of India for a drink. While lifting elbows through the evening, the Indian diplomat would have put across his government's point of view.

That no longer happens in Indian embassies and high commissions abroad, with rare exceptions. No wonder then, Modi and India now routinely get bad press in most parts of the world. Few officials from the Indian side now explain their government's point of view to the global media. So the foreign media delivers its judgment on India ex parte by default."

The fear of the backlash from the powers-that-be was so strong that even senior leaders avoided their journalist friends in public. Phone calls were made on WhatsApp to avoid tapping and tracing. No officer was open to meetings and no one gave official quotes to confirm or deny a story. For the government, especially the duo running it, journalists were enemies.

A prominent anchor, while interviewing a minister at a function, narrated how he had carried a series of stories criticising some decisions of the Congress government, and the then Prime Minister Manmohan Singh invited him to his office for a discussion on them. The Minister smiled and replied, "We do not believe in this because we respect your right to expression and your freedom of speech. You say whatever you want to say. And please forget that you will get any such invitation from there. The government is doing its work efficiently."

Social media was out and out against the Modi Sarkar. And Twitter trends were causing throbbing migraines to the government. It wanted complete control over content and any one posing a hurdle in its attempt was nothing but anti national and traitorous.

Twitter was quite active during these times. It first closed Kangana Ranaut's account because of her provocative tweets, and, later, labelled party spokesperson Sambit Patra's tweet as 'manipulated.' The government wanted the company to remove the manipulated tag from its star spokesperson's handle but Twitter took a stand. Twitter, it may be recalled, had earlier banned ex American President Donald Trump's account.

However, it was not as if the government was asking for something illegal. Moreover, if a legal provision is made then companies have to be abide by it. But the problem was lack of faith in the government. Users of social media were already up in arms against WhatsApp's revised policy of privacy that gave them no option other than agree to its right to share the user data with its parent company, Facebook. An exodus of user had started from WhatsApp to Telegram and other messaging apps.

However, people of the country had, by this time, started looking at everything with suspicion. They didn't trust the government to keep their data safe. The move to tame media giants so that they are forced to share data with government added to the suspicion.

People also looked at the state's action against WhatsApp and other social media platforms as its reaction to the steep fall in Sarkar's popularity on social media. It may be a coincidence that this regulatory framework of the government was conceived at a time when the Sarkar was no more a favourite on social media. It was rather being subjected to mockery, ridicule, taunts and jibes. Its YouTube videos and portions of speeches were subject of various memes which garnered more `likes` than the original speeches which had an overwhelming number of 'dislikes.' The laboriously built facade of infallibility had cracked when a single pebble hit it – the mishandling of Covid-19 pandemic. Repeated monologues on TV by Modi asking for positivity went in vain.

News channels acted on cue from the Sarkar and started debating on questions like, `Why are Twitter and WhatsApp above of the law of the land?` Simultaneously, they accused the agitating farmers of being super spreaders of the virus while ignoring massive electoral gatherings in poll-bound Bengal. An anchor asked its panellists, "How can you hold elections responsible for the spread of Covid? Are there any elections in Maharashtra and Chhatisgarh? They are worst on the Covid front." Another anchor asked the farmers, "You have become a major source of spread, why don't you wrap up your protest and come back after the virus is over?" Such unsolicited and sponsored suggestions were call of the day on the TV screens.

And finally amid the cacophony over the social media especially Twitter whom, the Sarkar found to be violating its instructions, an FIR was registered against the microblogging site and others including journalists and politicians for promoting communal hatred between religions by circulating a `fake and manipulated` video of an elderly Muslim man who was shown alleging in the clip that his perpetrators forced him to chant, "Vande Matram and "Jai Shri Ram." The FIR was registered under sections 153, 153-A, 295-A, 505 and 120-B of the Indian Penal Code. The police said that the elderly man Sufi Abdul Samad shown in the video was beaten by both the Hindus and Muslims for some amulets he gave them and which did not work as claimed by Samad. The case, police said, was of personal enmity and no communal angle was attached to it while certain individuals circulated without verifying the video with an ulterior motive to spread communal hatred.

Those booked included the social media site Twitter, news portal, The Wire and the fact checker of altnews Mohammad Zubair, journalist Rana Ayyub, writer Saba Naqvi and Congress leaders Sama Mohammad, Salman Nizami and Masqoor Usmani. It was one of the first punitive action against any social media site under the new IT rules. It happened on the same day, June 16, 2021, Twitter lost the protection granted to it as a third party intermediary under section 79 of the Information Technology Act. The government withdrew this protection after it said that the Twitter had deliberately chosen not to comply with the new intermediary guidelines even after numerous reminders. Union Minister for electronics and Information Technology Ravi Shankar Prasad slammed Twitter for its inconsistency in fighting the misinformation and fake news. Ironically, Prasad first expressed his outrage on the indigenous social media site Koo and then on the Twitter. It's history that Prasad was later shunted out of the ministry along with his a dozen colleagues.

15

The Mistaken Identity

Indira Gandhi's era taught Indian politics the grave consequences of declaring an emergency, a mistake no political party would dare repeat. Emergency remains a dark chapter, and linking it to every issue, big or small, would be a disservice to our political and historical awareness. However, even in opposition, the Congress has repeated this error on a minor scale. At a time when TV anchors' credibility has waned in ordinary households, and people are turning to YouTube journalists, the opposition, led by the Congress, has compiled a list of fourteen anchors to boycott. While this immediate action may stir some temporary upheaval in favor of the opposition, it risks being viewed as another misstep akin to the 'Emergency' in the future.

Anchors are often seen as magicians, wielding influence on TV channels, yet the treatment of these anchors had been overlooked until the opposition's bold decision to publicly announce the boycott list, which was seen as commendable yet could be counterproductive.

It must be remembered that speaking out isn't merely an individual or social act; it entails grappling with the political aftermath, which is never simple. The manner, content, and audience of one's speech are always scrutinised. Hence, today, those mindful of history's lessons are raising their voices. They understand that silence in critical moments can haunt for centuries. Throughout world history, there's been a struggle between those who speak and those who maintain silence.

Each era brings its own distinctiveness, and presently, it's characterised by outspokenness. However, in recent times, freedom of speech seemed restricted. There are "your anchors" and "our anchors," dividing lines have been drawn with the boycott of the anchors. Though it seemed inevitable—the anchors who once held the opposition accountable were now boycotted by the same opposition. This time, it was the opposition, not the ruling party, declaring the boycott. They have released a list, accompanied by formal portraits, declaring the boycott, stating that no member of the opposition alliance, the INDIA would participate in their programs.

The opposition especially the Congress seemed to have forgotten the lessons of history. In a program titled "Public Opinion Brotherhood," a senior BJP leader asserted that Indira Gandhi taught a crucial lesson to Indian politics—no party would ever declare an emergency again. The BJP leader was correct; they learned from Congress's history. Consequently, those speaking out today accused the BJP government of an undeclared emergency. An undeclared emergency is invisible, lacking in paper documents, stamps, or signatures. Its signs were apparent in the present, but it would not be documented in history. There won't be a specific date marked as the anniversary of an undeclared emergency.

Emergency is such a grim term that it starkly contrasts with any bright backdrop. Thus, associating it with every decision, big or small, would distort historical consciousness. Yet, Congress repeatedly made this mistake, this time under the leadership of the opposition alliance. Being in opposition isn't easy; it entails responsibility and accountability. Just earlier, you referred to Rahul Gandhi as an ascetic. Being in opposition is as challenging as being an ascetic. On one hand, there's the image of embracing in parliament, while on the other, there's the image of boycotting anchors. The "leader of Mohabbat" has been transformed into the "boycotter."

The integration of anchoring marked a pivotal shift in journalism's trajectory, signaling its demise. As the 20th century drew to a close, anchors seamlessly assimilated into Indian households, akin to the fandom surrounding Bollywood stars. Each household embraced their chosen anchor, fostering a culture that birthed the phenomenon of "prime time," revolutionising the media landscape. Gone were the days when mundane political happenings dominated headlines; now, the mere migration of an anchor from one faction to another became breaking news. Yet, these anchors now stand apart from their erstwhile affiliations.

The race to monopolise "prime time" saw anchors wielding their influence, captivating audiences amidst the plethora of channels available. While 24/7 channels filled the hours, one hour of "prime time" reigned supreme, later rebroadcast in the mornings and afternoons.

However, journalism paid the price for this fixation on ratings and star anchors. Initially embraced by some, fatigue set in, driving viewers back to traditional media sources in search of genuine news.

In essence, the presence of anchors often eclipsed genuine news, cloaked in the guise of spectacle and illusion. While newspapers diligently covered numerous stories across twelve pages, the hour-long programs hosted by these anchors amounted to mere noise. Viewers gradually discerned the charade, likening it to the staged disappearances orchestrated by these magicians, met with applause from a deceived audience.

As viewers awoke to the reality, they realised they were applauding for magicians who made critical issues vanish from public discourse, from inflation to unemployment, from crumbling infrastructure to failing healthcare. Consequently, viewers themselves began to disappear from TV screens, disillusioned, awaiting the return of substantive journalism.

Before imposing a boycott, the opposition should have evaluated the true standing of these anchors. Their predicament mirrors that depicted in Christopher Nolan's film "The Prestige," where the veneer of magic reveals a chronic ailment. Reality always prevails, irrespective of the illusion's allure, be it in language, thought, emotion, or the biased narratives spun by anchors. Every magic trick has its limit, and when exposed, only regret remains.

The opposition's boycott appeared to signal the end of an era, encapsulated by these fourteen individuals. However, it's reminiscent of a comedic spectacle rather than a substantive political move. The media institution, akin to a school, rewards exemplary conduct while addressing errant behavior. Anchors, once symbols of journalistic integrity, now shirk editorial responsibility, usurping the role of the editor as guardians of news. This shift has catalysed partisan journalism, eroding the collective and constitutional essence of journalism.

Ultimately, the elevation of anchors to the pinnacle of journalism has fostered a culture of sensationalism and bias. The opposition, by boycotting these anchors, inadvertently elevates them to the status of journalistic icons, which is nothing but a mistaken identity.

16

Agree or...!

The rampant use of the sedition law ultimately provoked a scathing judgement against the Central Government. The law was used indiscriminately on newsmen ranging from a small-time journalist like Pawan Jaiswal to the veteran of the field Late Vinod Dua.

The judgement came as a jolt to the government, as in their petition Telugu TV channels, TV5 and ABN, had challenged the FIR registered against them by the Andhra Pradesh police under sections 124 A, 153 A, and 505 of the Indian Penal Code. Among these sections, 124 A pertains to sedition that says any signs, visible representations, or words, spoken or written, that can cause hatred or contempt, or excite or attempt to excite disaffection against the government would come under the ambit of sedition. Needless to say that British colonial era provision was conceived to arm twist freedom fighters and to crush India's freedom movement.

The apex court stayed any coercive action against the channels. The channels were accused of telecasting an interview of a rebel MP Krishnam Raju in which he criticised the Chief Minister Y.S. Jagan Mohan Reddy for his handling of the pandemic. The police took suo motu action in registering the FIR on May 14, 2021. The point of worry was that of late this tendency of fixing rivals and critical journalists in false and baseless cases had spread to parties other than the BJP too.

The Supreme Court quashed the sedition case registered against a Padma Shri Awardee and former TV journalist who ran his own YouTube channel invoking a 59- year old verdict passed in 1962 and known as the Kedar Nath Singh judgement. The Supreme Court said that sedition case registered on the basis of strong words of disapproval against the ruling government cannot be considered seditious. The judgement was passed by a bench led by Justice U.U. Lalit. The judgement also said that for the sake of the freedom of speech of the journalists, they should be given protection from the accusations of sedition.

The judgement was exceedingly important for the journalists who were working under dire circumstances because of the sensitive nature of the government against any word of criticism. The Uttar Pradesh government under Yogi Adityanath was so sensitive that it registered a case against a journalist Pawan Jaiswal under 186 (obstructing a public servant from discharging his duties), 193 (false evidence), 120 B (criminal conspiracy) and 420 (cheating) after he made and circulated a video of a primary school at Shiur in Mirzapur district of the Uttar Pradesh where namak and roti was being served to the students under the midday meal scheme on August 22, 2019. The Yogi government's reaction to the story was the proverbial shooting the messenger as instead of taking stock of the grim state of affairs in the midday meal scheme, it arrested the newsman.

The judgment in Vinod Dua case quoted excerpts of the 1962 Kedar Nath Singh judgment. "Commenting in strong terms upon the measures or acts of government, or its agencies, so as to ameliorate the condition of the people or to secure the cancellation or alteration of those acts or measures by lawful means, that is to say, without exciting those feelings of enmity and disloyalty which imply excitement to public disorder or the use of violence is not sedition," it said.

A day before the quashing of Vinod Dua sedition case, the Supreme Court took a grim view of the way sedition law was being misused and took it on itself to review the colonial era sections of sedition under the Indian Penal Code. Earlier, on a number of occasions, analysts had been expressing concern over the way these provisions were being misused by the government to fix opponents.

A bench of Justice D.Y. Chandrachud, Justice L.N. Rao and Justice S.R. Bhat reportedly observed, "We are of the view that that the ambit and parameters of Sections 124 A, 153 A and 505 of the Indian Penal Code, 1860, would require interpretation, particularly in the context of the right of the electronic and print media to communicate news and information, even those that may be critical of the prevailing regime in any part of the nation."

Sedition cases, as per the National Crime Records Bureau, increased manifold in recent years. Reported data divulged that 93 cases of sedition were filed in 2019, an increase of 165 per cent from 35 cases recorded in 2016. During this period, 1,226 cases were also filed under the Unlawful Activities (Prevention) Act, a 33 per cent increase from 2016.

Much to the chagrin of the Sarkar's managers and thoughtless act of hurrying in to register a case against Dua, the judgement endorsed Dua view that he was raising an issue of great public concern. The judgement said, "The situation was alarming. Dua's views and statements can best be termed expressions of disapprobation of actions of the government and its functionaries so that the prevailing situation could be addressed quickly and efficiently. He was touching upon issues of great concern."

Dua in his YouTube video came down heavily on the government over the nationwide lockdown imposed at short notice. The video was released on March 30, 2020, when migrant labourers from Delhi, Mumbai and other states were headed to their homes in UP and Bihar on foot as the government had stopped all forms of public transport. The international media carried pictures and stories of unending stream of humans and their miseries on the highways. Surprisingly, more than a month after the video was released, an FIR was registered against Dua, first in Himachal Pradesh, and then in Delhi.

The government turned so intolerant to dissenting voices that a school was charged with sedition in Bidar of Karnataka. The school had staged a play against the Citizenship Amendment Act (CAA) in which a class 6 girl student had allegedly made uncharitable remarks against Prime Minister Narendra Modi. A report in the Times of India, June 11, 2020, said the police booked the student's mother and members of the school management, including the chairman on charges of sedition though the school denied having staged the play.

Subsequent to the Vinod Dua judgement, the Editors Guild of India too raised its voice against the sedition law and demanded it should be scrapped immediately.

Meanwhile, within days of the Vinod Dua judgement, Delhi High Court made a scathing commentary on the prevailing tendency of crushing dissent in the country while granting bail to three student activists whom the Delhi police booked under the stringent provisions of the Unlawful Activities (Prevention) Act. A year ago Delhi police registered an FIR against Pinjra Tod activists Natasha Narwal, Devangna

Kalita, students of Jawahar Lal Nehru university and student leader Asif Iqbal of Jamia Millia university for their alleged role in the Northeast Delhi riots in May 2020.

The court while granting them bail which was challenged in the Supreme Court by the Delhi police at an alarming speed, a bench of Justices Siddharth Mridul and Anup Jairam Bhambhani observed, "it seems, that in its anxiety to suppress dissent, in the mind of the State, the line between the constitutionally guaranteed right to protest and terrorist activity seems to be getting somewhat blurred." Newspapers reported though ostensibly anchors failed to take note of the judgement that set a benchmark for the democracy. The court also said that the allegations against the student leaders were based on stretched inferences and alarming hyperbolic verbiage. No wonder that the Delhi police rushed to challenge the judgement but failed to get any relief and the student activists were released on bail.

Ironically, it was not for the first time that the Sarkar came under allegations of treating dissent as sedition. The court also said that indiscriminate use of Unlawful Activities (Prevention) Act and its severe provisions would only trivialise them. But one only missed the story on TV news and had to wait for the newspapers to bring the contents of the scathing judgement to their homes in the morning.

17

The Great Divide

Ravish Kumar was the biggest casualty after the Adani Group took over NDTV in November 2022. He resigned soon after NDTV's founding couple, Prannoy and Radhika Roy, put in their papers after selling their stake in the channel.

Speculation on Ravish's resignation was rife for long due to his anti-Modi stance and the channel's take over by the Adani Group. He was ruling the social media and appeared to be taller than the organization he was working for. Though NDTV management never gave him full editorial control, Ravish became an iconic figure amongst his followers for his relentless campaign against the mainstream television platforms that he dubbed as godi media. In fact, if the mainstream media was one side of contemporary journalism, Ravish was the other side. Both had their own extreme point of view on the ruling dispensation.

"Seth ek patarkar kharid nahi paya to poora channel kharid liya. (When Seth (Adani) failed to buy a journalist, he purchased the entire channel)." The line set the narrative and Ravish trended on Twitter. Soon, millions subscribed to his yet to be launched YouTube channel in the post- NDTV scenario.

Ravish fought against attempts to isolate him and emerged as a powerful voice against the government, especially against

Prime Minister Narendra Modi. But he was also accused of bias on his evening programme Prime Time because he ostensibly took a one-sided, anti- establishment posture. He also railed against television channels for cuddling up with the Modi government and junking the media' role as a watchdog. His coinage godi media gained currency among the masses. There were several instances when common people raised slogans against mainstream television anchors — godi media wapas jao — during their live public telecasts.

However, those who followed his programme on YouTube closely knew that he hardly ever broke a story or conducted investigations into the alleged misdoings of the government. He largely quoted from the mainstream print media, especially The Indian Express and The Hindu, besides other newspapers and online portals. He however added punch to his programme with his satirical approach to issues, and also through his direct attack on Modi and his government. Since he was the only TV media personality to take a stand in the name of objective, analytical and fair journalism, he became a firm favourite of those who were either out of favour or disgruntled in the NDA government. A senior minister, who dissed him when in power, sang paeans of praise for Ravish when he was shunted out from the Modi cabinet.

Ravish though should be credited for exhorting news consumers to shun TV channels that preferred to lie comfortably with the government rather than report on it with professional honesty. The anti-godi sentiment quickly spiralled during the mainstream media's coverage of student protest at the Jawaharlal Nehru University in New Delhi. A visibly upset Aaj Tak anchor Anjana Om Kashyap was cornered outside the Bihar Vidhan Sabha with slogans of godi media wapas jao. Her terrified image on social media mirrored the public's loss of faith in electronic media.

The loss of credibility was inevitable because media had become a noisy arena for political parties' spokespersons to settle scores in a friendly match in which everybody was given a win-win situation. The anchors held these so-called debates at public places and exhorted the assembled public to welcome the spokespersons with applause. It was a bad version of a circus.

Ironically, Ravish's exit was so predictable that it did not stir controversy or even mild chatter on social media. It was taken for granted. News channels ignored it, while newspapers carried a small, single column, factual story. There were no professional obituaries written on his exit. Commentators, including those who had appeared on his programme frequently, preferred to keep their mouths shut on his resignation. He was only interviewed by an online portal, and perhaps one YouTube channel. He trended on Twitter though, like any other viral story, for full 15 minutes of fame before he joined the social media line up with those who had made similar exits from channels because of a hostile establishment.

Since 2014, the government made sure that it sidelined journalists. It brought them to the fore when they suited its convenience, like for staged interviews during election time. The standard procedure for such interviews was that the 'chosen' journalist was handed a questionnaire, the answers for which had already been written down for the VIP interviewee. The chosen one happily read out the list of questions and later claimed it to be ``a super exclusive," "explosive," "mega" or "bombastic" interview. It was painful to witness journalism at its lowest ebb.

On its part, journalism was deeply divided. It had also become personal. Journalists like Ravish Kumar lamented BJP's victory in 2022 UP Vidhan Sabha elections as a personal defeat. "It is our defeat. It is not their (BJP) victory but it is our defeat." On the other hand, the majority of TV channels announced gleefully that they had won. "We told you it would be a great victory. History made. Opposition crushed!" Such claims made it appear as if the mainstream media had turned the elections in favour of the ruling party!

Electronic journalism was thus passing through its most illusory phase where it believed that it could turn the tables in elections. Needless to say, they were fed this illusion by none other than the ruling party that blatantly used it to its benefit. There were courts ruling against such news channels, commentators writing against them, their own certain counterparts were revealing their real face on social media, and fact-checking teams of various platforms were exposing these channels, but they continued their work unabashedly.

Given the grave scenario, Rahul Gandhi, whose Bharat Jodo Yatra genuinely rattled the ruling party, pitied the anchors who were at the venue of his Yatra in Delhi. "Do not blame them for what they are doing by spreading hatred 24x7 on their channels. It's not their fault. Better identify the power behind them," he said.

He also recalled, "When I joined politics in 2004, these channels were full of praise for me and continued to be so until I started raising questions about farmers, poor and common man. The questions did not suit them and their bosses. Then they started a tirade against me." His precise point was that the government was run by two industrialists, Ambani and Adani, and everybody in the government was out to please them. He also accused the channels of spreading hatred by running a

24x7 Hindu-Muslim agenda. He minced no words to say that communal hatred was being spread at the behest of the BJP.

Rahul Gandhi could attack because objectivity was a luxury that none of the TV channels could afford. Those who followed them could easily tell which anchor would set what narrative and would take which side during the debate. A few of them were reserved for typical Hindu- Muslim debates and were followed by right wing believers.

The media tried to maintain the illusion of balancing their stories by getting versions of spokespersons of other political parties too, but they were seldom allowed to have their say. It finally began to boomerang when Opposition party spokespersons became strident about their right to speech and expression on such debates.

The Opposition alleged that the country was under an undeclared Emergency and press was under severe pressure. Official participants, when confronted with these allegations, reminded the Opposition of the Emergency under the rule of the Congress party. Surprisingly, even after a decade in power, BJP tried to win over various arguments on the strength of the follies of the previous Congress governments. It was clear that they did not have achievements of their own during their terms in power to counter the Opposition charges against it.

The government also claimed that the press was free under its rule. It said it exerted no direct or indirect pressures on it. But strangely, journalism also saw its worst ever phase under the Modi Government. Newspapers or channels, which the government felt were working against it, were denied advertisements and deleted from the list of invitees to government functions. All access for interviews or information was denied to even 'pliable journalist,' as Rahul Gandhi called them, who were part of godi media. The press was free but the door was shut on it by the government.

Newspapers that tried to question the government were raided by Income Tax Department, Enforcement Directorate and the Central Bureau of Investigation (CBI), etc. on flimsy grounds. When Dainik Bhasker exposed the government's inept handling of Covid-19 and tore apart forged figures of deaths due to the virus, Income Tax authorities arrived at the premises of the newspaper. Bhaskar was not an exception. There was a long list of news organisations that suffered due to their tough posture against the government. The Wire, NewsClick and the British Broadcasting Corporation (BBC), to name a few, were among those that faced the government's wrath.

News Click represented a culmination of dire circumstances. Established in 2009 by veteran journalist Prabir Purkayastha, who also served as its Editor, the news outlet encountered a significant setback when it became the subject of scrutiny by the Delhi Police, allegedly due to receiving foreign funding. The entity faced legal action under Sections 406, 420, and 120 B of the Indian Penal Code, as well as stringent provisions of the Unlawful Activities (Prevention) Act (UAPA) and Prevention of Money Laundering Act (PMLA), on grounds of purportedly disseminating pro-China propaganda. Notably, this marked the first instance where government sources purportedly exposed connections between the media and China.

Accusations stemmed from allegations that PPK NewsClick Studio Private Limited, the parent company of NewsClick, received funds amounting to Rs 9.59 crore from Worldwide Media Holdings LLC, based in the United States. The complaint, filed in August 2020, asserted that the investment was facilitated by inflating the company's share valuation to purportedly circumvent the prescribed 26 percent cap on foreign direct investment in digital media. Subsequently, reports surfaced, including from The New York Times and Al Jazeera, suggesting that these funds were provided by a US millionaire to NewsClick, purportedly resulting in coverage biased towards Chinese interests.

These allegations were vehemently refuted by both NewsClick and the implicated US individual. Concurrently, during the second term of Prime Minister Narendra Modi, bilateral relations between India and China had deteriorated, leading to mutual accusations and counter-accusations.

State agencies conducted raids on approximately 30 individuals associated with the media organization, including senior journalists. While these actions elicited outcry from the Editors Guild of India and the Press Club of India, their influence in advocating for journalistic integrity had diminished significantly, given the government's apparent disregard for their concerns. Opposition parties also condemned the government's actions, albeit without eliciting any substantive response. However, on May 15, 2024, the Supreme Court in a significant decision ordered release of Purkayastha stating that his arrest and remand under the draconian Unlawful Activities Prevention Act, 1967 (UAPA) were "invalid in the eyes of law."

Ironically, coinciding with these events, India's position on the World Press Freedom Index further declined, from 150th to 161st place. Despite this, the government maintained its stance, asserting the presence of a free press within the country, while dismissing the index's findings.

However, these agencies served their purpose well — they caused a dreadful quiet in the press. The government machinery, in fact, was so sure that it could dictate terms to the press that hand- outs of Information and Broadcasting Minister Anurag Thakur often carried a one-line `instruction': Pl carry on front page. The audacity was another first during Modi rule. Earlier, when Smriti Irani was the Information and Broadcasting Minister, the press had passed under a different kind of bad patch.

In sum, the decade of Modi rule gave a Ravish Kumar and an Arnab Goswami to this country. They are two sides of a bad partisan journalism coin. They are a unique, if not infamous, contribution of Modi era to journalism.

❑❑